A C

'I shall probably be unable to advise you so long as I don't know what you're talking about.' Amalfi said, impressed in spite of himself by the tone of high seriousness with which the Hevians spoke. 'Just what was the discovery that turned you back? What is the forthcoming event that you seem to dread?'

'Nothing less,' Retma said evenly, 'than the imminent coming to an end of time itself.'

By James Blish in Arrow Books

CITIES IN FLIGHT

1. They Shall Have Stars
2. A Life for the Stars
3. Earthman, Come Home
4. A Clash of Cymbals

—

A Case of Conscience

The Seedling Stars

James Blish

A CLASH OF CYMBALS

ARROW BOOKS

ARROW BOOKS LTD
3 Fitzroy Square, London W1

An imprint of the Hutchinson Publishing Group

London Melbourne Sydney Auckland
Wellington Johannesburg Cape Town
and agencies throughout the world

First published in Great Britain by
Faber and Faber 1959
Arrow edition 1974
Second impression August 1974

Made and printed in Great Britain
by The Anchor Press Ltd
Tiptree, Essex

ISBN 0 09 908660 3

Author's Note

This, the fourth and last volume of *Cities in Flight*, was first titled "The Triumph of Time," but that title disappeared—not without bowing to Swinburne—when it was found to resemble too closely that of another science-fiction novel on Faber and Faber's list for that season.

The old title, however, reflects the paradox which dictated the ending of the saga. The more I worked with my Okie cities, the more it seemed to me that they were becoming self-perpetuating entities whose histories, unlike the author's, could have no end—yet it is the primary law of the universe that nothing (least of all a sentient creature) can last forever. Time must triumph. It was up to me to show how, somehow.

This, in turn, posed me the question: How would people react if they knew, with absolute certainty, the exact moment when they would die? I had already put my very long-lived characters through nearly every other possible test; this one, it seemed to me, would reveal each one of them at last in his essential nakedness. And, cruelly but inevitably, there would be young people too who would have to face the question.

This is the only part of *Cities in Flight* (except for about a third of the first volume) that never appeared in a magazine; its U.S. book publisher got it into print too quickly to permit its serialization. The one magazine editor who saw the manuscript, however, proposed to retitle it "The Augustinian Age" (after the one reference to St. Augustine in the volume) and cut from it all the material about Jorn the Warrior of God; so my escape was fortunate.

Here, then, is how the cities passed. I shall miss them.

JAMES BLISH

New York
1964

CHRONOLOGY

A.D.

2012 Bliss Wagoner elected Senator (D.) from Alaska. Dr. Guiseppi Corsi drummed out of the U.S. Bureau of Standards as a security risk.

2013 Joint Senate-House Committee on Space Flight launches the Jupiter Project. Department of Health, Education, Welfare and Security underwrites international conference on degenerative disease.

2015 Investigating subcommittee of the Senate Finance Committee votes to investigate the Bridge.

2016 Construction of the Proserpine Station begun.

2018 Bliss Wagoner re-elected. Discovery of ascomycin.

2019 Publication of the report on the Bridge investigation. Discovery of the Dillon–Wagoner graviton-polarity generator.

2020 Second investigation of the Bridge. Flight of Wagoner. The Believer Riots. The Orders of Extradition. Fall of the Bridge.

2021 Escape of the "Colonials" from the Jovian system. Trial and death of Wagoner. Death of Corsi, under questioning.

2022 The MacHinery–Erdsenov Agreement. The Cold Peace.

2027 Assassination of MacHinery. The Erdsenov Proclamation.

2032 Assassination of Erdsenov. The Terror. The Hamiltonian Exodus.

2039 Banning of space flight and all associated sciences on Earth, by the Krushchevgrad Proclamation.
2105 Fall of the West (an agreed arbitrary date).
2289 First colonial contact with the Vegan Tyranny.
2310 The Battle of Altair, first engagement of the Vegan War.
2375 Rediscovery of the spindizzy. Escape from Earth of the Thorium Trust's Plant No. 8.
2394 Height of the Earth Exodus. Rape of Thor V by the Interstellar Master Traders (*orig.* Gravitogorsk–Mars).
2413 Investment of Vega. Battle of the Forts. Scorching of the Vegan system by the Third Colonial Navy, under Adm. Hrunta.
2451 Alois Hrunta found guilty *in absentia* of atrocities and attempted genocide by the Colonial Court, Judge Schmitz presiding.
2464 Battle of BD 40°4048′. Alois Hrunta declares himself Emperor of Space.
2522 Collapse of the Bureaucratic State. The Police Interregnum. Proclamation of amnesty to the colonists. Beginning of the Empty Years.
2998 Birth of John Amalfi.
3089 Amalfi becomes mayor of Manhattan. Poisoning of Alois Hrunta. Balkanization of the Hruntan Empire.
3111 Manhattan leaves the Earth. Arpad Hrunta installed as Emperor of Space.
3200 Birth of Mark Hazleton. Anti-Earth pogrom in the Malar system; colonization of the Acolyte cluster.
3301 Manhattan violates its contract on Epoch; deFord is shot, and Hazleton becomes city manager.
3548 Escape of Squadron 32 of the Hruntan Navy from the Battle of Procyon. Founding of the Duchy of Gort.
3571 Interception of the war between Gort and Utopia.
3602 Reduction of Gort and Utopia by the Earth police. Second Hamiltonian Exodus. Death of Arpad Hrunta; dissolution of the Empire. Escape of Manhattan.

3844 The crossing of the Rift. First contact with the planet of He.

3850 The tipping of He; beginning of the first intergalactic crossing.

3900 Collapse of the germanium standard.

3905 Battle of the Jungle, in the Acolyte cluster. Lt. Lerner named Acolyte-Regent. Beginning of the March on Earth.

3910 Acolyte-Regent Lerner proclaims himself Emperor of Space.

3911 The flight of Hern VI. Annihilation of the Acolyte fleet by the Earth police. Death of Emperor Lerner, under an overdose of wisdom-weed, in a slum on Murphy.

3913 The Battle of Earth. Last stand of the Vegan Tyranny.

3917 Hern VI leaves the galaxy.

3918 Manhattan leaves the galaxy. Re-election of Mayor Amalfi.

3925 Passage of the anti-Okie bill.

3944 Discovery of the Interstellar Master Traders. Colonization of the Greater Magellanic Cloud.

3948 The Battle of the Blasted Heath. Destruction of IMT by the Earth police. Abandonment by Earth of the Clouds.

3949 Founding of New Earth.

4000 Assimilation by the Web of Hercules of the Earth culture; emergence of the Milky Way's IVth great civilization. The return of He.

4002 The Jehad of Jorn. Conquest and recovery of New Earth.

4004 The Ginnunga-Gap.

Bismillahi 'rrahmani 'rrahim
When the day that must come shall have come suddenly,
None shall treat that sudden coming as a lie:
Day that shall abase! Day that shall exalt!
When the earth shall be shaken with a shock,
And the mountains shall be crumbled with a crumbling,
And shall become scattered dust,
And into three bands shall ye be divided: . . .
Before thee have we granted to a man a life that shall last forever:
If thou then die, shall they live forever?
Every soul shall taste of death: . . .
But it shall come on them suddenly and shall confound them; and they shall not be able to put it back, neither shall they be respited.

THE KORAN;
Sura LVI, Sura XXI

CONTENTS

PROLOGUE

. . . Thus we have seen that Earth, a planet like other civilized worlds, having a score of myriads of years of atmosphere-bound history behind her, and having begun manned local space-flight in approximately her own year 1960, did not achieve importance on a galactic scale until her independent discovery of the graviton polarity generator in her year 2019. Her colonials made first contact with the Vegan Tyranny in 2289, and the antagonism between the two great cultures, one on its way down, the other rapidly developing, culminated in the Battle of Altair in 2310, the first engagement of what has come to be known as the Vegan War. Some sixty-five years later, Earth launched the first of the fleet of space-cruising cities, the "Okies", by which it was eventually to dominate the galaxy for a long period, and in 2413 the long struggle with the Vegans came to an end with the investment of Vega itself, and the Battle of the Forts. The subsequent scorching of the Vegan system by the Third Colonial Navy, under Admiral Alois Hrunta, prompted Earth proper to indict its admiral *in absentia* for atrocities and attempted genocide. The case was tried, also *in absentia*, by the Colonial Court; Hrunta was found guilty, but refused to submit to judgment. An attempt to bring him in by force brought home for the first time the fact that the Third Colonial Navy had defected to him almost *en masse* and resulted in 2464 in the Battle of BD 40°4048′. Both sides suffered heavy losses, but there was no other outcome, and Hrunta subsequently declared himself Emperor of Space—the first of many such gimcrack "empires" which were to spawn on the fringes of Earth's jurisdiction during the so-called Empty Years. This period officially began in 2522 with the collapse of local government on Earth—the Bureaucratic State, dating from 2105—which after a brief police interregnum allowed the now large numbers of Okie cities to develop in effectual anarchy, a condition very well suited to their proliferation of trade routes throughout the known and unknown galaxy.

We have already discussed the collapse under its own weight of the Hruntan Empire and the final reduction of the fragments by the recrudescent Earth police during the period 3545–3602. We have stressed this relatively minor aspect of Earth history not because it was at all unusual, but because it was typical of the balkanization of Earth's official power during the very period when its actual power was greatly on the rise. Our discussion of the history of one of the Okie cities, New York, N.Y., which began its space-flying career in 3111 and thus overlapped much of the history of the Hruntan Empire, may be compared to illustrate the difference in the treatment accorded by Earth to her two very different children, empires and Okies, and history shows the wisdom of the choice; for it was the wide-ranging Okies who were to make the galaxy an orchard for Earth for a relatively long period, as such periods go in galactic history.

Customs and cultures pronounced officially dead have, however, a way of stirring again long after their supposed interment. In some instances, of course, this is simply a reflex twitch; for example, though the grandiose collapse of the Earth culture certainly can be said to have begun during the Battle of the Jungle in the Acolyte cluster in 3905, we find only five years later the Acolyte-Regent, a Lt. Lerner, proclaiming himself Emperor of Space; but the Acolyte fleet, already considerably cut up by its encounter with the Okies in the jungle, was annihilated by the Earth police on their arrival a year later, and Emperor Lerner died that same year in a slum on a tenth-rate Acolyte planet named Murphy from an overdose of wisdomweed. On a larger scale, the Battle of Earth in 3913, in which Earth found herself pitted against her own Okie cities, was marked also by an unexpected resurrection of the Vegan Tyranny, whose secretly constructed and long-wandering orbital fort chose this moment to make its last bid for galactic power. Its failure was a repetition in miniature of the failure of the entire Vegan Tyranny, despite superior force of arms, in any conflict with the Earthmen, who were far better chessmasters; the Vegans characteristically left prediction to computers, which lack the ability to make long intuitive leaps, as well as the decisiveness to act upon them.

The Okie city which had outplayed the Vegan orbital fort in the game of thinking ahead, our type-city New York, was far enough ahead of its own culture to have left the galaxy by 3918 for the Greater Magellanic Cloud. It left behind an Earth which in 3925 cut its own throat as a galactic power with the passage of the so-called anti-Okie Bill. Though the Magellanic planet which New York colonized in 3944 was in 3949 christened New Earth, the earlier date of 3925 marks the passing of Earth from the stellar stage. Already there were reaching out from one of the galaxy's largest and most beautiful star-clusters the first tentative strands of that strange culture called the Web of Hercules, which was destined to become the Milky Way's IVth great civilization. And yet once more a civilization which from every historical point of view had to be pronounced dead refused to stay entirely buried. The creeping, inexorable growth of the Web of Hercules through the heart of the galaxy was destined to be interrupted by that totally revolutionary, totally universal physical cataclysm now known as the Ginnunga-Gap; and though it is due entirely to the Web of Hercules that we still have records of galactic history before that cataclysm, and thus a continuity with the universe's past surely unprecedented in all the previous cycles, we must note, with more than a little awe, the sudden and critical reappearance of Earthmen in this timeless moment of chaos and creation, and the drastic and fruitful exeunt which they wrote for themselves into the universal drama.

ACREFF-MONALES:
The Milky Way: Five Cultural Portraits

1

NEW EARTH

In these later years it occasionally startled John Amalfi to be confronted by evidence that there was anything in the universe that was older than he was, and the irrationality of his allowing himself to be startled by such a truism startled him all over again. This crushing sensation of age, of the sheer dead weight of a thousand years bearing down upon his back, was in itself a symptom of what was wrong with him—or, as he preferred to think of it, of what was wrong with New Earth.

He had been so startled while prowling disconsolately through the grounded and abandoned hulk of the city, itself an organism many millennia older than he was, but —as befitted such an antiquity—now only a corpse. It was, indeed, the corpse of a whole society; for nobody on New Earth now contemplated building any more space-cruising cities or in any other way resuming the wandering life of the Okies. Those of the original crew on New Earth, spread very thin among the natives and their own children and grandchildren, now looked back on that entire period with a sort of impersonal, remote distaste, and would certainly recoil from the very idea of returning to it, should anyone have the bad manners to broach such a notion. As for the second and third generations, they knew of the Okie days only as history, and looked upon the hulk of the flying city that had brought their parents to New Earth as a fantastically clumsy and outmoded monster, much as the pilot of an ancient atmospheric liner might have regarded a still more ancient quinquireme in a museum.

No one except Amalfi even appeared to take any interest in what might have happened to the whole of Okie society back in the home lens, the Milky Way galaxy of which the two Magellanics were satellites. To give them credit, finding out what had happened would in any event have been an almost impossible task; all kinds of broadcasts—literally millions of them—could be picked up easily from the home lens if anyone cared to listen, but so much time had elapsed since the colonization of New Earth that sorting these messages into a meaningful picture would require years of work by a team of experts, and none could be found who would take any interest in so fruitless and essentially nostalgic a chore. Amalfi had in fact come into the city with the vague notion of turning the task over to the City Fathers, that enormous bank of computing and memory storage machines to which had been entrusted all the thousands of routine technical, operational and governmental problems of the city when it had been in flight. What Amalfi would do with the information when and if he got it he had no idea; certainly there was no possibility of interesting any of the other New Earthmen in it, except in the form of half an hour's idle chatter.

And after all, the New Earthmen were right. The

Greater Magellanic Cloud was drawing steadily away from the home lens, at well over 150 miles per second—a trifling velocity in actuality, only a little greater than the diameter of the average solar system per year, but symbolic of the new attitude among the New Earthmen; people's eyes were directed outward, away from all that ancient history. There was considerably more interest in a nova which had flared into being in intergalactic space, somewhere beyond the Lesser Magellanic, than there was in the entire panoply of the home lens, visibly though the latter dominated the night sky from horizon to horizon during certain seasons of the year. There was, of course, still space flight, for trade with other planets in the little satellite galaxy was a necessity; the trade was conducted for the most part in large cargo hulls, and there were a number of larger units such as mobile processing plants which still needed to be powered by gravitron-polarity generators or "spin-dizzies"; but for the most part the trend was toward the development of local, self-sufficient industries.

It was while he was setting up the City Fathers for the problem in analysis of the million-fold transmission from the home lens, alone in what had once been his Mayor's Office, that Amalfi had suddenly had thrown at him the fragment from the writings of a man dead eleven centuries before Amalfi had been born. Possibly the uttering of the unexpected fragment had been simply an artifact of the warming-up process—like most computers of their age and degree of complexity, it took the City Fathers two to three hours to become completely sane after they had been out of service for a while—or perhaps Amalfi's fingers, working with sure automatism even after all these years, had been wiser than his head, and without the collusion of Amalfi's consciousness had built into the problem elements of what was really troubling him: the New Earthmen. In either event, the quotation was certainly apposite:

"If this be the whole fruit of the victory, we say: if the generations of mankind suffered and laid down their lives; if prophets and martyrs sang in the fire, and all the sacred tears were shed for no other end than that a race of creatures of such unexampled insipidity should succeed, to protract *in saecula saeculorum* their contented and inoffensive lives—why, at such a rate, better lose than win the battle, or at all events better ring down the curtain before the last act of the play, so that a business that began so importantly may be saved from so singularly flat a winding-up."

"What was *that*?" Amalfi barked into the microphone.

"AN EXTRACT FROM *The Will to Believe* BY WILLIAM JAMES, MR. MAYOR."

"Well, it's irrevelant; get your bottles and firecrackers back on the main problem. Wait a minute—is this the Librarian?"

"YES, MR. MAYOR."

"What's the date of the work you quoted?"

"1897, MR. MAYOR."

"All right. Switch out and hook into the analytical side of the loop; you've no business at the output end for this problem."

A flowmeter needle bobbed upward as the drain of the library machine on the circuit was discontinued for a moment, then dipped again. He did not proceed with the project for a while, however, but instead simply sat and thought about the fragment that the machines had offered him. There were, he supposed, a few unreconstructed Okies still alive on New Earth, though the only one that he knew personally was John Amalfi. He himself had no special nostalgia *qua* nostalgia for all the history he had outlived, for he could hardly forget that it had been by his foreplanning that New Earth had been founded. And for a period of perhaps four years there had been plenty to occupy his mind: the discovery that the planet, then unnamed, was at once the refuge and the feudal fief of a notorious pack of bindlestiffs calling itself Interstellar Master Traders—better known in the home lens simply as "the Mad Dogs"—had raised a considerable obstacle to colonization, the solution of which obviously needed to be drastic, and was. But the destruction of IMT in 3948 in the Battle of the Blasted Heath had left Amalfi at long last without problems and without function, and he had subsequently found himself utterly unable to become used to living in a stable and ordered society. The James quotation almost perfectly summarized his feelings about the Okie citizens who had once been his charges, and their descendants; he had of course to excuse the natives, who knew no better and were finding the problems of self-government an unprecedented challenge after their serfdom under "the Mad Dogs".

Local space travel, he knew very well, was no solution for him; one planet in the Cloud was very like another, and the Cloud itself was only 20,000 light years in diameter—a fact which made the Cloud extremely convenient to organize from one administrative centre, but a fact of no significance whatsoever to a man who had once shepherded his city across 280,000 light years in a single flight. What he missed, after all, was not space, but instability itself, the feeling of being on the way to an unknown destination, unable to predict what outlandish surprises might be awaiting him at the next planetfall.

The fact of the matter was that longevity now hung on him like a curse. An indefinitely prolonged life span had been a prerequisite for an Okie society—indeed, until the discovery of the anti-agathic drugs early in the twenty-first century, interstellar flight even with the spindizzy had been a physical impossibility; the distances involved were simply too great for a short-lived man to compass at any finite speed—but to be a virtually immortal man in a stable society was to be as uninteresting to one's self, for Amalfi at least, as an everlasting light bulb; he felt that he had simply been screwed into his socket and forgotten.

It was true that most of the other former Okies had seemed able to make the change-over—the youngsters in particular, whose experience of star wandering had been limited, were now putting their long life expectancies to the obvious use: launching vast research or development projects the fruition of which could not be expected in under five centuries or more. There was, for example, an entire research team now hard at work in New Manhattan on the overall problem of anti-matter. The theoretical brains of the project were being supplied largely by Dr. Schloss, an ex-Hruntan physicist who had boarded the city back in 3602 as a refugee during the reduction of the Duchy of Gort, a last surviving polyp of the extinct Hruntan Empire; administration of the project was in the hands of a comparative youngster named Carrel, who not so long ago had been the city's co-pilot and ranking understudy to the City Manager. The immediate objective of the project, according to Carrel, was the elucidation of the theoretical molecular structures possible to anti-material atoms, but it was no secret that the most of the young men in the group, with the active support of Schloss himself, were hoping in a few centuries to achieve the actual construction, not only of simple chemical compounds—that might come about in a matter of decades—of this radical type, but a visible, macroscopic artifact composed entirely of anti-matter. Upon the unthinkably explosive object they would no doubt paint, Amalfi surmised, had they by that time also composed an antimaterial paint and something to keep it in, the warning *Noli me tangere.*

That was all very well; but it was equally impossible for Amalfi, who was not a scientist, to participate. It was, of course, perfectly possible for him to end his life; he was not invulnerable, nor even truly immortal; immortality is a meaningless word in a universe where the fundamental laws, being stochastic in nature, allow no one to bar accidents, and where life no matter how prolonged is at bottom only a local and temporary discontinuity in the Second Law of Thermo-dynamics. The thought, however, did not occur to Amalfi; he was not the suicidal type. He had never felt less tired, less used-up, less despairing than he felt today; he was simply snarlingly bored, and too confirmed in his millennia-old patterns of thought and emotion to be able to settle for a single planet and a single social order, no matter how utopian; his thousand years of continuous translation from one culture to another had built up in him an enormous momentum which now seemed to be bearing him irresistibly toward an immovable inertial wall labelled, NO PLACE TO GO.

"Amalfi! So it's you. I might have guessed."

Amalfi shot the "hold" switch closed convulsively and swung around on his stool. He had, however, recognized the voice at once from centuries of familiarity. He had heard it often since somewhere around 3500, when the city had taken its owner on board as chief of the astronomy section: a testy and difficult little man with a deceptively mild manner who had never been precisely the chief astronomer that the city needed, but who had come through in the pinches often enough to prevent the City Fathers from allowing him to be swapped to another Okie city during the period when such swaps were still possible for Amalfi's town.

"Hello, Jake," Amalfi said.

"Hello, John," the astronomer said, peering curiously at the set-up board. "The Hazletons told me I might find you prowling around this old hulk, but I confess I'd forgotten about it by the time I decided to come over here. I wanted to use the computation section, but I couldn't get in—the machines were all shuttling back and forth on their tracks and coupling and uncoupling like a pack of demented two-hundred-ton ballet dancers. I thought maybe one of the kids had wandered in up here in the control room and was fooling with the boards. What are you up to?"

It was an extremely pointed question which, up to now, Amalfi had not asked himself. Even to consider answering Jake by describing the message-analysis project was to reject it; not that Jake would care one way or the other, but to Amalfi's inner self the answer would be an obvious blind. He said:

"I don't quite know. I had an urge to look around the place again. I hate to see it going to rust; I keep thinking it must still be good for something."

"It is, it is," Jake said. "After all, there are no computers quite like the City Fathers anywhere else on New Earth, let alone anywhere else in the Magellanics. I call on them pretty frequently when there's anything really complicated to be worked on; so does Schloss, I understand. After all, the City Fathers know a great deal that nobody else around here can know, and old though they are, they're still reasonably fast."

"I think there must be more to it than that," Amalfi said. "The city was powerful, is powerful still; the central pile is good for a million years yet at a minimum, and some of the spindizzies must still be operable—providing that we ever again find anything big enough to need all the lifting power we've got concentrated down below in the hold."

"Why should we?" the astronomer said, obviously not very much interested. "That's all past and done with."

"But is it? I keep thinking that no machine of the sophistication and complexity of the city can ever go quite out of use. And I don't mean just marginal uses, like occasionally consulting the City Fathers, or tapping the pile for some fraction of its total charge. This city was meant to fly, and by God it ought to be flying still."

"What for?"

"I don't know, exactly. Maybe for exploration, maybe for work, the kind of work we used to do. There must be some jobs in the Cloud for which nothing less than a machine of this size is suitable—though obviously we haven't hit such a job yet. Maybe it would be worth cruising and looking for one."

"I doubt it," Jake said. "Anyhow, she's gotten pretty tumbledown since we had our little difference with IMT, what with all those rocket bombs they threw at us—and letting her be rained on steadily ever since hasn't helped, either. Besides, I seem to remember that that old 23rd St. spindizzy blew for good and all when we landed here. I hardly think she'd stir at all now if you tried to lift her, though no doubt she'd groan a good deal."

"I wasn't proposing to pick up the whole thing, anyhow," Amalfi said. "I know well enough that that couldn't be done. But the city's *over*-sophisticated for a field of action as small as the Cloud; there's a lot you could leave behind. Besides, we'd have a great deal of difficulty in scaring up anything more than a skeleton crew, but if we could rehabilitate only a part of her, we might still get her aloft again——"

"Part of her?" Jake said. "How do you propose to section a city with a granite keel? Particularly one composed as a unit on that keel? You'd find that many of the units that you most needed in your fraction would be in the outlying districts and couldn't be either cut off or transported inward; that's the way she was built, as a piece."

This of course was true. Amalfi said: "But supposing it could be done? How would you feel about it, Jake? You were an Okie for nearly five centuries; don't you miss it, a little, now?"

"Not a bit," the astronomer said briskly. "To tell

you the truth, Amalfi, I never liked it. It was just that there was no place else to go. I thought you were all crazy with your gunning around the sky, your incessant tangles with the cops, and your wars, and the periods of starvation and all the rest, but you gave me a floating platform to work from and a good close look at stars and systems I could never have seen as well from a fixed observatory with any possible telescope, and besides, I got fed. So I was reasonably satisfied. But do it again, now that I have a choice? Certainly not. In fact, I only came over here to get some computational work done on this new star that's cropped up just beyond the Lesser Cloud; it's behaving outrageously—in fact, it's the prettiest theoretical problem I've encountered in a couple of centuries. I wish you'd let me know when you're through with the boards; I really do need the City Fathers, when they're available."

"I'm through now," Amalfi said, getting off the stool. As an afterthought, he turned back to the boards and cleared the instruction circuits of the problem he had been setting up, a problem which he now knew all too well to be a dummy.

He left Jake humming contentedly as he set up his nova problem, and wandered without real intention or direction down into the main body of the city, trying to remember it as it had been as a living and vibrant organism; but the empty streets, the blank windows, the flat quiet of the very air under the blue sky of New Earth, were like an insult. Even the feeling of gravity under his feet seemed in these familiar surroundings a fleering denial of the causes and values to which he had been given most of his life; a smug gravity, so easily maintained by sheer mass, and without the constant distant sound of spindizzies which always before—since his distant, utterly unrememberable youth—had signified that gravity was a thing made by man, and maintained by man.

Depressed, Amalfi quit the streets for the holds of the city. There, at least, his memory of the city as a live entity would not be mocked by the unnaturally natural day. But that in the long run proved to be no better. The empty granaries and cold-storage bins reminded him that there was no longer any need to keep the city stocked for trips that might last as much as a century between planet-falls; the empty crude-oil tanks rang hollowly, not to his touch, but simply to his footfall as he passed them; the empty dormitories were full of those peculiar ghosts which not the dead, but the living leave behind when they pass, still living, to another kind of life; the empty classrooms, which were, as was quite usual with Okie cities, small, were mocked by the memory of the myriads of children which the Okies were now farrowing on their own planet, New Earth, no longer bound by the need to consider how many children an Okie city needs and can comfortably provide for. And down at the threshold of the keel itself, he encountered the final sign and sigal of his forthcoming defeat: the fused masses of two spindizzies ruined beyond repair by the landing of 3944 on the Blasted Heath. New spindizzies, of course, could be built and installed, the old yanked out; but the process would take a long time; there were no graving docks suitable for the job on New Earth, since the cities were extinct. As was the spirit.

Nevertheless, in the cold gloom of the spindizzy hold, Amalfi resolved to try.

"But what on earth do you expect to gain?" Hazleton said in exasperation, for at least the fifth time. "I think you're out of your mind."

There was still no one else on New Earth who would have had the temerity to speak to Amalfi quite like that; but Mark Hazleton had been Amalfi's city manager ever since 3301 and knew his former boss very well. A subtle, difficult, lazy, impulsive and sometimes dangerous man, Hazleton had survived many blunders for which the City Fathers would have had any other city manager shot—as, indeed, they had had his predecessor shot—and he had survived, too, his often unwarranted assumption that he could read Amalfi's mind.

There was surely no other ex-Okie on New Earth who might be as likely to understand Amalfi's present state of mind, but Hazleton was not at the moment giving a very good demonstration of this. For one thing, he and his wife Dee—the girl from a planet called Utopia who had boarded the city about the same time that Dr. Schloss had, during the reduction of the Duchy of Gort—had perhaps forgotten that an Okie tradition forbade the mayor of an Okie city to marry or have children, and that Amalfi as the mayor of New York since 3089 was conditioned beyond redemption to this state of mind; and in particular would not welcome being surrounded by the children and grandchildren of his city manager at any time, and particularly not when what he most urgently needed was advice from someone who remembered the traditions well enough to understand why another man might still be clinging to them.

It was one of Mark's virtues, however, that at his

best he tended to react more like a symbiote than a truly separate entity. When the children made graceful exits soon after dinner, Amalfi knew that it was at Hazleton's behest. He also knew it was not because Hazleton even faintly suspected his friend's discomfiture in the presence of so many fruits of the settling-down process; it was just that the city manager had intuited Amalfi's need for a conference and had promptly set one up, scuttling Dee's social time-table without a qualm.

The children charged their unseasonably early departure to the grandchildren's impending bedtimes, although Amalfi knew that when the whole clan came to dinner they customarily made a great occasion of it, and all stayed the night in the adjoining building, a beehive of bedrooms where the Hazletons had raised their numerous family; the current Hazleton dwelling consisted mostly of the huge social room where they had just dined. Now that the meal was over, Amalfi just barely kept from fidgeting while all the procession of big and little Hazletons made their manners. Even the youngest had each to make his farewell speech to the great man, identifying his inconsiderable self; their parents had long since learned in their own childhoods that the busy Mr. Mayor would not trouble himself to remember which was which.

It never occurred to Amalfi to admire the children's concealment of their disappointment at leaving so precipitately, since he did not realize that they were disappointed. He simply listened without listening. One middle-sized boy caught his attention mainly because from the moment he had arrived Amalfi had noticed that the child had kept his eyes riveted on the guest of honour. It was disconcerting. Amalfi suspected he had forgotten to don some essential garment or to doff some trace of his party preparations. When the child who had caused him to rub his chin and smooth his eyebrows and finger his ears to see if there were still soapsuds in them spoke up, Amalfi paid attention.

"Webster Hazleton, sir, and I hope to be seeing you again on a matter of the greatest importance," the boy said. He said it as if he had been rehearsing it for weeks, with a ringing conviction that almost impelled Amalfi to fix an appointment then and there.

Instead, he growled: "Webster, eh?"

"Yes, sir. I was put on the Great List to be born when Webster wanted off."

Amalfi was considerably jolted. So long ago as that! Webster had been the pile engineer who had elected to leave the city just before the landing on Utopia, around 3600. Of course it had taken a long time to fill up the gaps in the city's roster after the murderous attempt of the bandit cities to prevent fulfilment of their contract on He, and the considerable losses in boarding the plague city in the Acolyte jungle; and then there had been so many girls born at first. This Webster had been an unconscionably long time in coming, though. He could not be more than fourteen, from the looks of him.

Dee intervened. "Actually, John, Web arrived a long time after the Great List was abandoned. It pleases him to have his patron citizen, that's all, just like in the old days."

The boy turned his clear brown eyes on Dee briefly, and then, as if dismissing her from their male universe, he said: "Good night, sir." Amalfi bridled a little. Nobody could write Dee off, not even Amalfi; he knew; once he had tried.

The procession continued while he lapsed back into inattention, and eventually he found himself closeted with Dee and Mark—if closeted was the word in a room so large and echoing with so many strong personalities. The aura of furious domesticity remained behind on the Hazleton hearth, and came between Amalfi and what he was trying to say, so that his exposition was unwontedly stumbling; and it was then that Hazleton had asked him what he expected to gain.

"Gain?" Amalfi said. "I don't expect to gain anything. I'd just like to be aloft again, that's all."

"But, John," Dee said. "Think about it a minute. Suppose you do succeed in persuading a few people from the old days to go in with you. It all doesn't have any meaning any more. You'll just turn yourself into a sort of Flying Dutchman, sailing under a curse, going nowhere and doing nothing."

"Maybe so," Amalfi said. "The picture doesn't frighten me, Dee. As a matter of fact, it gives me a sort of perverse satisfaction, if you must know. I shouldn't mind becoming a legend; at least that would fit me back into history again—give me a role to play comparable to roles I've played in the past. And besides, I'd be aloft again, which is the important thing. I'm beginning to believe that nothing else is important to me any more."

"Does it matter what's important to us?" Hazleton said. "For one thing, such a venture would leave the Cloud without a mayor. I don't know how important that is to you any more—I seem to remember that it was pretty important to you back when we were on our way here—but whether it matters to you any more or not, you ran for the job, you connived for it, you even rigged the election—Carrel and I were supposed to be the only candidates, and the office we were running for was city manager, but you had the City Fathers hornswoggled into believing that it was a mayoralty election, so of course they elected you."

"Do you want the job?" Amalfi said.

"Gods of all stars, no! I want you to keep it. You exercised considerable ingenuity to get it, and I'm not alone in expecting you to hold it down now that you've got it. Nobody else is bidding for the job; they expect you to handle it, as you undertook to do."

"Nobody else is running for it because they wouldn't know what to do with it after they got it," Amalfi said steadily. "I don't know what to do with it myself. The office of mayor is an anachronism in this Cloud. Nobody has asked me to do anything or to say anything or to appear anywhere or to be in any other way useful in I don't know how many years. I occupy an honorary office, and that's all. As everybody knows, you are the man that is actually running this Cloud, and that's as it should be. It's high time you took over in name, as well as in fact. I've given everything I could give to the initial organizing job, and my talents are unsuitable to the situation as it now stands; everybody on New Earth knows that, and it would be healthier if they'd put a name to it. Otherwise, Mark, how long could I be allowed to go on in the job? Apparently for ever, under your present assumptions. This is a new society; suppose I should go right on being its titular leader for another thousand years, as is entirely possible? A thousand years during which a new society continues to give lip-service to the same old set of attitudes and ideas that I represented when they meant something? That would be unsane; and you know it. No, no, it's high time you took over."

Hazleton was silent for quite a long time. At last he said:

"I can see that. In fact, I've thought of it several times myself. Nevertheless, Amalfi, I have to say that this whole proposition distresses me a good deal. I suppose the matter of the mayoralty would settle itself out almost automatically; that wasn't a real objection. What bothers me is the exit you're contriving for yourself, not only because it's dangerous—which it is, but that wouldn't make any difference to you and I suppose it shouldn't make any difference to me—but because it's dangerous to no purpose."

"It suits my purposes," Amalfi said. "I don't see that there are any other purposes to be suited, at this juncture. If I did, I wouldn't go, Mark; you know that; but it seems to me that I am now, for the first time in all my life, a free agent; hence I may now do what I will do."

Hazleton shrugged convulsively. "And so you may," he said. "I can only say that I wish you wouldn't."

Dee bowed her head and said nothing.

And the rest was left unsaid. That Dee and Mark would be personally bereaved if Amalfi persisted on his present course, for their different reasons, was an obvious additional argument which they might have used, but they came no closer to it than that; it was the kind of argument which Hazleton would regard as pure emotional blackmail, precisely because it was unreasonably powerful, and Amalfi was grateful to him for not bringing it to bear. Why Dee had not was more difficult to fathom; there had been a time when she would have used it without a moment's hesitation; and Amalfi thought he knew her well enough to suspect that she had good reasons for wanting to use it now. She had been waiting for the founding of New Earth for a long time, indeed, almost since she had come on board the city, and anything that threatened it now that she had children and grandchildren should provoke her into using every weapon at her command; yet, she was silent. Perhaps she was old enough now to realize that not even John Amalfi could steal from her an entire satellite galaxy; at any event, if that was what was on her mind, she gave no inkling of it, and the evening in Hazleton's house ended with a stiff formality which, cold though it was, was far from the worst that Amalfi had expected.

The whole of the residential area to Amalfi's eyes swarmed with pets. Those to whom freedom to run was paramount frisked and scuttered in the wide lanes. Few of them ventured on to the wheelways, and those who did were run down instantly, but four-footed animals were a constant and undignified hazard to walkers. By day raffish dogs stopped just short of bowling strangers over, but leaped to brace forepaws on the shoulders of anyone they knew—and everyone, includ ing, seemingly, all the dogs of New Manhattan, knew Amalfi. An occasional svengali from Altair IV—originally a rare specimen in the flying city's zoo, but latterly force-budded in New Earth labs during the full-fertility programme of 3950, when every homesteader's bride had her option of a vial of trilby water or a gemmate svengali and frequently wound up with both among the household lares and penates; half-plant, half-animal, even nowadays a not infrequent pet—took the breeze and hunted in the half-light of dawn or dusk. A svengali lay bonelessly in mid-lane and fixed its enormous eyes on any moving object until something small enough and gelid enough to ingest might blunder near. Nothing suitable ever did, on New Earth. The two-legged victim tended to drift helplessly into that hypnotic stare until the starer got stepped on; then the svengali turned mauve and exuded a protective spray which might have been nauseating on Altair IV, but on New Earth was only euphoric. Sudden friendships, bursts of song, even a brief and deliriously happy crying jag might ensue, after which the shaken svengali would undulate back indoors to rest up and be given, usually, a bowl of jellied soup.

By night in the walkways of New Manhattan, it was cats, catching with sudden claw at floating cloak or fashionable sandal-streamer. Through the air of the town sizeable and brightly coloured creatures flew and glided: singing birds, squawking birds, talkers and mutes, but pets every last one of them. Amalfi loathed them all.

When he walked anywhere—and he walked almost everywhere, now that the city's aircabs were no more—he more than half-expected to have to free himself from the embraces of a burbling citizen or a barking dog before he got where he was going. The half-century-old fad for household pets had arisen after the landing, and after his effectual abdication. What time-wasting quirk had moved so many pioneers' descendants to adopt the damnable svengalis as pets was beyond Amalfi.

He made it home from the Hazletons' without any such encounter; instead, it rained. He wrapped his cloak more tightly around him and hastened, muttering, for his own square uncompromising box of a dwelling before the full force of the storm should be let loose; his house and grounds were sheltered by a 0·02 per cent spindizzy field—the New Earthmen called the household device a "spindilly", a name which Amalfi loathed but put up with for the sake of, as Dee had once put it, "not knowing enough to come out in the rain". He had growled at her so convincingly for that that she had never brought up the subject again, but she had put her fingers on it all the same.

Amalfi reached his entrance lane and laid his palm on the induction switch which softened the spindilly field just enough to let him through in a spatter of glistening drops, and noted with the grim dissatisfaction that was becoming natural to him that the storm had slacked off and would be over in minutes. Inside, he made a drink and stood, rubbing his hands, looking about him. If his house was an anachronism, well, he liked it that way, in so far as he liked anything on New Earth.

"What's wrong with me?" he thought suddenly. "People's pets are their own business, after all. If practically everybody else likes weather, what difference does it make if I don't? If Jake doesn't even take an interest, nor Mark either for that matter——"

He heard the distant, endlessly comforting murmur of the modified spindizzy under his feet alter momentarily; someone else had chosen to come in out of the rain. His visitor had never been there at that hour before, and had indeed never been there before alone, but he knew without a moment's doubt who had followed him home.

2

NOVA MAGELLANIS

"You'll have to make me more welcome than that, John," Dee said.

Amalfi said nothing. He lowered his head like a bull contemplating a charge, spread his feet slightly, and clasped his hands behind him.

"Well, John?" Dee insisted gently.

"You don't want me to go," he said baldly. "Or, you suspect that if I do go, Mark just may throw up the managership and New Earth along with it and take off with me."

Dee walked slowly all the way across the room and stood, hesitating, beside a great deep cushion. "Wrong, John, on both counts. I had something else altogether in mind. I thought—well, I'll tell you later what I thought. Right now, may I have a drink?"

Amalfi was forced to abandon his position, which by being so firm had imparted a certain strength to his desire to oppose her, in order to play host. "Did Mark send you, then?"

She laughed. "King Mark sends me on a good many errands, but this wouldn't be a very likely one for him." She added bitterly: "Besides, he's so wrapped up in Gifford Bonner's group that he ignores me for months on end."

Amalfi knew what she meant: Dr. Bonner was the teacher-leader of an informal philosophical group called the Stochastics; Amalfi hadn't bothered to inform himself in detail on Bonner's tenets, but he knew in general that Stochasticism was the most recent of many attempts to construct a complete philosophy, from esthetics to ethics, using modern physics as the metaphysical base. Logical positivism had been only the first of those; Stochasticism, Amalfi strongly suspected, would be far from the last.

"I could see something had been keeping his mind off the job lately," he said grimly. "He might do better to study the doctrines of Jorn the Apostle. The Warriors of God control no less than fifteen of the border planets right now, and the faith doesn't lack for adherents right here on New Earth. It appeals to the bumpkin type—and I'm afraid we've been turning out a lot of those lately."

If Dee recognized this as in part a shaft at the changes in New Earth's educational system which she had helped to institute, she showed no sign of it.

"Maybe so," she said. "But I couldn't persuade him, and I wonder if you could either. He doesn't believe there's any real threat; he thinks that a man simple-minded enough to be a Fundamentalist is too simple-minded to hold together an army."

"Oh? Mark had better ask Bonner to tell him about Godfrey of Bouillon."

"Who was——?"

"The leader of the First Crusade."

She shrugged. Possibly only Amalfi, as the only New Earthman who had actually been born and raised on

Earth, could ever have heard of the Crusades; doubtless they had been unknown on Utopia.

"Anyhow, that isn't what I came here to talk about, either."

The wall treacher opened and floated the drinks out. Amalfi captured them and passed one over silently, waiting.

She took her glass from him but, instead of sinking down with it as he had half-pictured her doing, she walked nervously back to the door and took her first sip as if she might put it aside and be leaving at any moment.

He discovered that he did not want her to go. He wanted her to walk some more. There was something about the gown she was wearing——

That there were fashions again was a function of being earthbound. One simple utilitarian style had sufficed both men and women all their centuries aloft when there had been the unending demands of the city's spaceworthiness to keep all hands occupied. Now that the ex-Okies were busily fulfilling Franklin's law that people will breed to the point of overpopulating any space available to them, they were also frittering away their time with pets and flower-gardens and fashions that changed every time a man blinked. Women were floating around this year of 3995 in diaphanous creations that totalled so much yardage a man might find himself treading on their skirts. Dee, however, was wearing a simple white covering above and a clinging black tubular affair below that was completely different. The only diaphanous part of her outfit was a length of something gossamer and iridescent that circled her throat under a fold of the white garment and hung down between her still delicate, still gently rounded breasts, as girlish in appearance as the day Utopia had sent her out to New York, in a battleship, to ask for help.

He had it. "Dee, you looked just as you look now when I first saw you!"

"Indeed, John?"

"That black thing——"

"A sheath-skirt," she interpolated helpfully.

"—I noticed it particularly when you came aboard. I'd never seen anything like it. Haven't seen anything like it since." He refrained from telling her that during all the centuries he had loved her, he had pictured her in that black thing, turning to him instead of Hazleton. Would the course of history have been any different, had she done so? But how could he have done anything but reject her?

"It took you long enough to notice it tonight," she said. "I had it made up especially for this evening's dinner. I've been tired of all this float and flutter for a year. Essentially I'm still a product of Utopia, I guess. I like stern clothes and strong men and a reasonably hard life."

She was certainly trying to tell him something, but he was still adrift. The situation was impossible, on the face of it. He was not in the habit of discussing fashion with his best and oldest friend's wife at an hour when all sensible planet-bound pioneers were abed. He said: "It's very pretty."

To his astonishment, she burst into tears. "Oh, *don't* be stuffy, John!" She put the glass down and reached for her cloak.

"All right, Dee." Amalfi put the cloak out of her

reach. "Your 'King Mark' sounds reasonably stern and hard. Suppose you sit down and tell me what this is all about."

"I want to go with you, John. You won't be the mayor of New York, you won't be bound by the old rules, if you take the city aloft now. I want—I want to——"

It was weeks before he got her to state that ultimate desire. They had talked without ceasing after that blundering beginning. When it finally penetrated his cautious bald head that the message all his senses had been clamouring from the moment of her arrival was not another daydream from the chilly past, but warm actuality, he had folded her in his arms and they had been silent for a time. But then the flow of words began again and could not be checked. They had reminisced endlessly of how-it-might-have-beens and even of certain ways it had been. He was amazed to discover that she had taken into her household however briefly every companion whose bed he had honoured during the officially celibate years; in her position as First Lady of New Earth, during the intensive family years, she could have installed twenty nursemaids simultaneously without attracting undue notice, just as she launched every new fashion and many of the fads that made New Earth what it was. That Dee had been cruelly bored had simply never occurred to him.

But she told him the full tale of that discontent, more indeed than he wanted to hear. They quarrelled like giddy young lovers—except that their first and worst quarrel followed a complaint he could have wept to hear wrung from her.

"John," she said, "aren't you ever going to take me to bed?"

He spread his hands in exasperation. "I'm not at all sure I want to take Mark's wife to bed. Besides," he added, knowing he was being cruel, "you've already had it. You've pumped every woman I resorted to in half a thousand years. I should think I would bore you in actuality as much as everything else does."

Their reconciliations were not much like those of young love; they were more and more like the creeping home of a rebellious daughter to her father's arms. And still he held off. Now that he had for the taking what he had only dreamed of wanting for so many years, he made the Adamic discoveries all over again: there is wanting the unobtainable, and there is the obtaining of desire, and the greater of these is the wanting. Especially since the object of desire always turns out to exist only in some other universe, to be mocked by actuality.

"You don't believe me, John," she said bitterly. "But it's true. When you go, I want to go with you—all the way, don't you understand? I want to—I want to bear you a child."

She looked at him through a film of tears—somehow he had never, in all the centuries of fancy, imagined or seen her in tears, but the actuality wept as predictably as New Earth's skies—and waited. She had shot her bolt, he saw. This was the supreme thing that Dee Hazleton wanted to give him.

"Dee, you don't know what you're saying! You can't offer me your girlhood all over again—that's irretrievably Mark's, and you know it. Besides, I don't want——"

He stopped. She was weeping again. He had never wanted to hurt her, although he knew he had done so unintentionally more times than he would ever know.

"Dee, I've *had* a child."

Now she was listening, wide-eyed, and he winced as he saw pity take the place of resentment. He laid the encysted pain bare like a surgeon before her. "When the population balance shifted after the landing and there were all those excess females—remember? Do you also remember the artificial insemination programme? They asked me to contribute. The good old argument against it was supposed to be by-passed by the assurance that I'd never know which children carried my genes—only the doctors supervising the programme would know. But there was an unprecedented wave of miscarriages and stillbirths—and some survivors that shouldn't have survived, all with the same set of . . . disadvantages. I was told about it; as mayor, I had to decide what was to be done with them."

"John," she whispered. "No. Stop."

"We were taking over the Cloud," he continued implacably. Presenting him with a wizened, squalling, scarlet, normal baby boy was one favour she could not do him, and there was no way to tell her so but this. "We couldn't afford bad genes. I ordered the survivors . . . dealt with; and I had a brief conference with the genetics team. They had planned not to tell me—they were going to keep up the farce, like good-hearted dolts. But I'd been in space too long; my germ plasm is damaged beyond hope; I am no longer a contributor. Do you understand me, Dee?"

Dee tried to draw his head down on her breast.

Amalfi moved violently away. It irritated him unreasonably that she still thought she had anything to give him.

"The city was yours," she said tonelessly. "And now it's grown up and gone away and left you. I saw you grieving, John, and I couldn't bear it—oh, I don't mean that I was pretending. I love you, I think I always have. But I should have known that the time for us had gone by. There's nothing at all left for me to give you that you haven't had in full measure."

She bowed her head, and he stroked her hair awkwardly, wishing it had never begun, since it had to end like this. "And what now?" he said. "Now that life with father has turned out to be nothing more than that? Can you leave home again and go to Mark?"

"Mark? He doesn't even know I've been . . . away. As his wife, I'm dead and buried," she said in a low voice. "Living seems to be a process of continually being born again. I suppose the trick is to learn how to make that crucial exit without suffering the trauma each time. Good-bye, John."

She didn't look as if she were being too successful at mastering the trick, but he made no move to help her. She was going to have to find her own way back; she was beyond his aid now.

He thought that what she had said was probably the truth—for a woman. For a man, he knew, life is a process of dying, again and again; and the trick, he thought, is to do it piecemeal, and ungenerously.

For the first time in weeks, he walked the streets of New Manhattan again. He had never felt so utterly done with the purpose he had sowed in his people. Now that it was coming to fruition, he urgently needed to be seeking some purpose far removed from theirs.

Inevitably, he found himself leaving cats, birds, svengalis, dogs and Dee for the dilapidated streets of the Okie city. He was almost all the way down to the banks of the City Fathers, when a suspicion that he was again being followed turned into a certainty. For a panic moment he feared it might be Dee, spoiling both her exit and his; but it was not.

"All right, who is it?" he said. "Stop skulking and name yourself."

"You wouldn't remember me, Mr. Mayor," a frightened voice said in several registers at once.

"Remember you? Of course I do. You're Webster Hazleton. Who's your friend? What are you doing here in the old city? It's off limits for children."

The boy drew himself up to his full height.

"This is Estelle. She and I are in this together." Web appeared to have some difficulty in going on. "There's been talk—I mean, Estelle's father, he's Jake Freeman, kind of hinted about it—that is, if the city's really going up again, Mr. Mayor——"

"Maybe it is. I don't know yet. What of it?"

"If it is, *we want on*," the boy said in a rush.

Amalfi had had no further plans to try and convert Jake, who certainly appeared to be as lost a cause as Hazleton himself; but the Freeman-Hazleton partnership represented by Web and Estelle meant that he would have to broach the subject again to Jake sooner or later. Of course it was out of the question that the children should be allowed to go—and yet it was not within the bounds of fairness to forbid them out of hand, without knowing what their elders thought of it. Children had gone adventuring on Okie cities many a time before; but of course that had been back in the old days, when the cities had been as well equipped as any earthbound community to take good care of them, at least most of the time. Every thread he touched these days, it seemed to Amalfi, had knots in it.

Temporarily, however, the fates allowed him to shelve that part of the problem; for Jake was waiting for him again in the computation section, in a state of excitement so febrile that the sight of his daughter and Web tagging behind Amalfi barely raised his eyebrows.

"You're just in time," he said as though there had been some prior appointment. "You recall the nova I was talking to you about? Well, it isn't a nova at all, and at this point it's no longer an astronomical problem; in fact, it's your problem."

"What do you mean?" Amalfi said. "If it isn't a nova, what is it?"

"Just what I was asking myself," Jake said. One of his more irritating failings was his inability to get to a point by any but a pre-selected route. "I have a remarkable collection of spectrographs for this thing; if you looked at them without any clue as to what they were, you'd think they represented a stellar catalogue, rather than a single object—and a catalogue containing stars from all over the Russell diagram, too. On top of which, all of them show a blue shift in the absorption lines, particularly in the lines contributed by New Earth's own atmosphere, which made no sense whatsoever, up to now."

"It still doesn't make any sense to me," Amalfi admitted.

"All right," Jake said, "try this on for size: when the spectra turned out to be far too dim for an object of the apparent magnitude of this thing—remember, it's been getting brighter all the time—I asked Schloss and his crew to neglect anti-matter long enough to do a wave-trap analysis of the incoming light. It turns out to be about seventy-five per cent false photons; the thing must be leaving behind a tremendous contrail, if we were only in a position to see it——"

"Spindizzies!" Amalfi shouted. "And under damn near full deceleration! But how could an object that size—no, wait a minute; do you actually know the size yet?"

The astronomer chuckled, a noise which from Jake never failed to remind Amalfi of a demented parrot. "I think we have the size, and all the rest of the answers, at least as far as astronomy is concerned," he said. "The rest, as I said, is your problem. The thing is a planetary body, roughly seventy-five hundred miles in diameter, and much closer than we thought it was—right now, in fact, it's actually inside the Greater Magellanic, and coming our way, directly for the system of New Earth. The change in spectra simply means that it's shining by the reflected light of the different suns it's passing, and the blue shift in the Frauenhofer lines strongly suggests an atmosphere very much like ours. I don't know offhand what that reminds you of, but I know what it should remind you of—and the City Fathers agree with me."

Web Hazleton could contain himself no longer. "I

know, I know! It's the planet He! It's coming home! Isn't that it, Mr. Mayor?"

The boy knew his city history well; nobody from the old days could have been confronted with such a set of data as Jake had just trotted out without responding with the same wild surmise. The planet He had been one of the city's principal jobs of work, the outcome of which, for very complicated reasons, had entailed the installation on the planet itself of a number of spindizzies sufficient to rip He from her orbit around her home sun and send her careening, wholly out of control, out of the galaxy and into intergalactic space. The city had been carried a considerable distance with her, enabling it to re-enter the galaxy far away from any area where New York, N.Y., was being actively sought by the cops, but it had been a near thing. She, herself, presumably, had been hurtling toward the Andromeda galaxy ever since that moment in 3850 when she and the city had parted company, each vanishing to the other as abruptly and finally as a blown-out candle-flame.

"Let's not jump to conclusions," Amalfi said. "The tipping of He took place only a century and a half ago—and at that time the Hevians didn't have the technology or the resources to master controlled spindizzy flight; in fact, they weren't very far from being savages. Smart savages, I grant you, but still savages. Is this planet that's coming our way truly dirigible, or don't you know yet?"

"It looks that way," Jake said. "That's what first tipped me off that there was something unnatural about the object. It kept changing velocity and line of flight erratically—in fact, in a totally irrational way, unless one assumed that the changes were in fact rational. Whoever they are, they know enough to prevent that world of theirs from zigging when they want to zag. And they're headed our way, Amalfi."

"Have you made any attempt to get in touch with them, whoever they are?" Amalfi said.

"No, indeed. In fact, I haven't even told anybody else about it yet. Not even Mark. Somehow it struck me as peculiarly your baby."

"That was just a waste of pussyfooting, Jake. Dr. Schloss isn't an idiot; surely he can read his own figures as well as you can and draw obvious conclusions from the very question you asked him; he must have told Mark by now, and a good thing, too. Mark is probably calling your object right now; let's go directly up to the control room and find out."

They made an oddly assorted procession through the haunted streets of the Okie city: the bald-headed keg-chested mayor with his teeth deeply sunk in a dead cigar,. the bird-like and slightly crestfallen astronomer, the bright-eyed skipping youngsters now darting ahead of them, then falling behind to wait to be shown the way. Their eagerness moved Amalfi unexpectedly, bringing home to him the realization that their dream of the city back in flight had always been, like this, a very fragile one; and that this incoming dirigible planet, whatever else it might portend, would probably put the quietus to it, serious business and the dull cold morning light it thrived in being immemorially fatal to dreams.

On an impulse, he stopped at a station that he knew and called for an aircab, partly, he assured himself, to see whether or not the City Fathers still considered that service worth maintaining at this stage in the city's long death. In due course one came, to the obvious delight of the children, leaving Amalfi with the rueful realization that his had not been a fair test; a million years from now, with the last ergs of energy remaining in the pile, the City Fathers would of course still send a cab for the mayor; if he wanted to know whether or not the entire garage was still alive, he would have to ask the City Fathers directly.

But Web and Estelle were so delighted at soaring through the silent canyons of the city in the metal and crystal bubble, and in exploring the limited and very respectful repartee of the Tin Cabby, that they fell entirely off their precarious adolescent dignity with squeals of laughter, alternating with gasps of not very real alarm as the cab cut around corners and came close to grazing the structures of the city which familiarity had worn smooth to the point of contempt inside the Tin Cabby's flat little black box of a brain. It was, in a way, a shame that, as the cab sank slowly to the plaza before City Hall, the youngsters were unable to make out, even had they known where to look for it, the graven letters of the city's ancient motto—MOW YOUR LAWN, LADY?—if only for the sense it might have given them of the reason why Okie cities once flew; but the motto had become unreadable a long time ago, as its meaning had become obliterated soon after. Only the memory remained to remind Amalfi that were the city ever to go aloft again—which, suddenly, he did not even believe—it would not be for the purpose of mowing lawns for hire; there were no more; that was all over and done with.

The control room in City Hall muted the children

considerably, as well it might, for no one much below the age of a century had ever been allowed in it before, and the many screens which lined its walls had seen events in a history unlikely to be matched for drama (or even simple interest) in any imaginable future saga of New Earth. In this dim stagnant-smelling room the very man who was with them now had watched the rise and fall of a galaxy-dominating race—of which, to be sure, these children were genetically a part, but whose inheritors they could never be; history had passed them by.

"And don't touch anything," Amalfi said. "Everything in this room is alive, more or less. We've never had the time to disarm the city totally; I'm not even sure we'd know how to go about it now. That's why it's off limits. You'd better come stand behind me, Web and Estelle, and watch what I do; it'll keep you out of reach of the boards."

"We won't touch anything," Web said fervently.

"I know you won't, intentionally. But I don't want any accidents. Better you learn how to run the board from scratch; come stand right here—you too, Estelle—and call your grandfather's house for me. Touch the clear plastic bar—that's it, now wait for it to light up. That lets the City Fathers know that you want to talk to somebody outside the city; that's very important; otherwise they'd give you a long argument, believe you me. Now you see the five little red buttons just above the bar; the one you touch is number two; four and five are ultraphone and Dirac lines, which you don't need for a local call. One and three are inside trunk lines, which is why they're not lit up. Go ahead, push it."

Web touched the glowing red stud tentatively. Over his head, a voice said: "Communications."

"Now, it's my turn," Amalfi said, picking up the microphone. "This is the mayor. Get me the city manager, crash priority." He lowered the microphone and added: "That requires the Communications section to scan for your grandfather along all of the channels on which he's known to be available, and send him a 'call-in' signal wherever he may be; New Earth Hospital has much the same call-in system for its doctors."

"Can we hear him being called?" Estelle said.

"Yes, if you like," Amalfi said. "Here, take the microphone, and put your finger on the two-button as Web did. There."

"Communications," the invisible speaker again said briskly.

"Say, 'Reprise, please'," Amalfi whispered.

"Reprise, please," the girl said.

Immediately the air of the ancient room was filled with a series of twittering pure tones and chords, as though every shadow hid a bird with a silver throat. Estelle almost dropped the microphone; Amalfi took it from her gently.

"Machines don't call for people by name," he explained. "Only very complicated machines, like the City Fathers, are able to speak at all; a simple computor like the Communications section finds it easier to use musical tones. If you listen a while, you'll begin to hear a kind of melody; that's the code for Web's grandfather; the harmonies represent the different places where the computer is looking for him."

"I like it," Estelle said. At the same instant the

pipings of the invisible birds came to an end with a metallic snap, and Mark Hazleton's voice said in the middle of the air: "Boss, are you looking for me?"

Amalfi lifted the microphone back to his lips with a grim smile, the children instantly forgotten.

"You bet I am. Are you on top of this dirigible planet which seems to be heading for us?"

"Yes; I didn't know you were interested. In fact, I didn't know that it was a planet instead of a star until yesterday, when Schloss and Carrel came in to see me about it." Amalfi threw Jake a meaningful glance. "I gather you're calling me from the city; what do the City Fathers think?"

"I don't know, I haven't talked to them," Amalfi said. "But Jake is here, and he's come to the obvious conclusion, as I'm sure you have. What I want to know is, have you or Carrel made any attempt to communicate with this object?"

"Yes, but I can't say that it's been very fruitful," Hazleton's voice said. "We've called them four or five times on the Dirac, but if they've answered us, it's gotten lost in the general babble of Dirac 'casts we're surrounded with from the home galaxy. It puzzles me a little bit; they do seem to be homing on us, without any question, but it's hard to imagine what kind of signal from us they could be using to guide on."

"Do you really think that this is He come back again?" Amalfi said cautiously.

"Yes, I think I do," Hazleton said, with apparent equal caution. "I don't see what other conclusion one could come to with the data as they stand now."

"Then use your head," Amalfi said. "If this really is He, you'll never be able to reach it with a Dirac 'cast.

While we were on He, we never even let the Hevians hear a Dirac 'cast, or see a Dirac transmitter; they had no reason to suspect that any such universal transmitter even existed, or could exist. And if by the same token this is *not* He, but some exploring vessel coming in toward us for the first time from another galaxy, and out of an entirely different culture from any we know, then it's obvious that they cannot have the Dirac, otherwise they would have heard every one of the millions of Dirac messages which have gone out from our galaxy since the day they found the device. Try the ultraphone instead."

"He didn't have the ultraphone either, when last we saw it," Hazleton's voice said amusedly. "And if we don't know how to drive an ultraphone carrier through a spindizzy screen, I very much doubt that they do. If we're going to go all the way back to methods of communication as primitive as that, shouldn't we first try wig-wagging?"

"I think probably there is an ultraphone message from that planet on its way here," Amalfi said. "It would be the part of common sense to precede such a flight as that planet is conducting into so densely populated an area as the Greater Magellanic Cloud with a general identification signal, which you could hardly do with a Dirac signal in any event; a signal which is received uniformly everywhere simultaneously with its being sent is not a proper beacon signal. It doesn't matter whether this is He or a visitor coming to us from the entirely unknown; they will be sending some sort of pip in advance, which they would absolutely have to do by ultraphone, there being no other way to do it, and if this requires them to work out a way to punch an ultraphone signal through a spindizzy screen, then they will have done so and you should be listening for it; and you can put a return signal through the same hole." He took a deep breath. "At the very least, Mark, stop wasting my time telling me it's impossible before you've even tried it."

"I tell *you*," Webster Hazleton said under his breath and turned a bright scarlet. Behind him, Estelle's father chortled alarmingly on the edge of his metaphorical cracker-barrel.

The riot act, however, had been becoming less and less effective with Hazleton in the past few decades, as Amalfi knew well; perhaps it dated from Hazleton's new preoccupation with the Stochastics, about which Amalfi had not known until Dee had brought it up; or perhaps—though this was a much less attractive possibility—from an awareness in Hazleton, paralleling Amalfi's own, of Amalfi's growing impotence on New Earth. "Nevertheless," Hazleton said gravely, "I will raise one further objection, boss, if I may. Even supposing that they are putting out an ultraphone beam we can tie to, they're still roughly fifty light-years away; by the time they hear anything we say to them by ultraphone and get a message back to us the same way, we'll be seventy-five years into the next millennium."

"True," Amalfi admitted. "Which means we'll have to send a ship. I'm all for taking ten years or so about full contact, anyhow, since we really have no idea what it is we're confronted with, and we may need to lay in some armaments. But you'd better tell Carrel to stand ready to fly me out there no later than the beginning of next week, and in the meantime, try to eavesdrop on whatever transmission our visitor is broadcasting. I'll attend to the answering part later from shipboard."

"Right," Hazleton said, and switched out.

"Can we go too?" Web demanded immediately.

"What do you say to that, Jake? These kids were all for going with me on board the city, too."

The astronomer smiled and shrugged. "Wherever she gets the taste for spaceflight from, it can't be from me," he said. "But I knew she was going to ask sooner or later. It's an experience she'll have to have behind her before she's very much older, and I don't know of any commander in two galaxies that she'd be safer with. I think my wife will concur—though she's as uneasy about it as I am."

Web cheered; but Estelle only said, in a tone of the utmost practicality:

"I'll go home and get my svengali."

3

THE NURSERY OF TIME

Even from half a million miles out, it was already plain to Amalfi that the planet of He had undergone a vast transformation since he had last seen it, back in 3850. The Okies had first encountered that planet six years earlier, the only fertile offspring of a wild star then swimming alone in a vast starless desert, not one of the normal star-free areas between spiral arms of the galaxy, but a temporary valley called the Rift, the mechanics of whose origin lay shrouded impenetrably in the origins of the universe itself.

Even at first sight, it had been apparent that the history of He had been more than ordinarily complicated. It had then been an emerald-green world, covered with rank jungle from pole to pole, a jungle which had almost completely swamped out what had obviously been a high civilization not many years before. The facts as they emerged after landing turned out to be complex in the extreme; it was highly probable that there was not another planet in the galaxy which had undergone so many fatal and unlikely accidents. The Hevians had fought them all doggedly, but by the time the Okies had arrived they had realized that nothing less than a miracle could help them now.

For Hevian civilization, the Okies had been that

miracle, giving the Hevians mastery over their own local and considerable banditry, and killing off the planet-wide jungle, in the only way possible: by abruptly and permanently changing the climate of He. That this geological revolution had had to be accomplished by putting the whole planet into uncontrolled flight out of the galaxy was perhaps unfortunate, but Amalfi did not think so at the time. He had formed a high opinion of the shrewdness and latent technological ability underlying the Hevian ceremonial paint and feathers, and did not doubt that the Hevians would learn the necessary techniques for preserving their planet as an abodc of life well before the danger point would be reached. After all, the Hevians had been great once, and even after the long battle with the jungle and each other they had still had such sophistications as radio, rockets, missile weapons and supersonics when the Okies had first encountered them; and during the brief period that the Okies had been in contact with them, they had snapped up such Middle Ages and Early Modern techniques as nuclear fission and chemotherapy. Besides, there had been the spindizzies, some from the city, some new-built, but all necessarily left behind and in full operation; studied with the eye of intelligence, they could not but provide the Hevians with clues to many potent disciplines which they would have little difficulty putting to work once the jungle was gone; in the meantime, the machines would maintain the atmosphere of the planet and its internal heat even in the most frigid depths of intergalactic space; it would be the darkness of those gulfs, which the Hevians could mitigate but could hardly abolish, which would kill off the jungle.

Nevertheless, Amalfi had hardly expected to see the return of He, under wholly controlled spindizzy drive, in barely a century and a half, still faintly, patchily blue-green with cultivation under cloud-banks which glared a brilliant white in the light of a nearby Cepheid variable star. That the wandering body was He had been settled back home on New Earth as soon as Hazleton had been able to identify the wanderer's advance ultraphone beacon, as Amalfi had predicted; and hardly five minutes after Carrel had brought his ship out of spindizzy drive within hailing distance of the new planet, Amalfi had himself spoken to Miramon, the very same Hevian leader with whom the Okies had dealt one hundred and fifty years ago—to the mutual astonishment of each that the other was still alive.

"Not that I myself should have been surprised," Miramon said, from the head of his great council table of black, polished, oily wood. "After all, I myself am still alive, to an age beyond the age of all the patriarchs in our recorded history; which in turn is only a small fraction of the age you gave us to understand you had attained when first we met you. But old habits of thought die hard. We were able to isolate and purify only a few of the anti-agathics produced by our jungle, acting on the hints you had given us, before the jungle died off and the plants which produced those drugs did not prove cultivatable under the new conditions, so we had no choice but to search for ways to synthesize these compounds. We were forced to work very fast, and happily the search was successful by the third generation, but in the meantime the existing supply had sufficed to keep only a few of us alive beyond what we still think of as our normal lifespans. Hence to most of our population, Mayor Amalfi, you are now only a legend, an immortal man of infinite wisdom from beyond the stars, and I have been unable to prevent myself from coming to think of you in much the same way."

Though he still wore in his topknot the great black barbaric saw-toothed feather of his authority, the Miramon before Amalfi today bore little resemblance to the lithe, supple, hard-headedly practical semi-savage who had once squatted on the floor in Amalfi's presence, because chairs were the uncomfortable prerogatives of the gods. His skin was still firm and tanned, his eyes bright and darting, but, though his abundant hair was now quite white, he had settled into that period of life, neither youth nor age, characteristic of the man who goes on anti-agathics only when somewhat past "natural" middle age. His councillors—including Retma, of Fabr-Suithe, which in Amalfi's time had been a bandit town which had been utterly destroyed during the last struggle before He took flight, but which now, rebuilt in ceremonial pink marble, was the second city of all He—mostly wore this same look. There were one or two who obviously had not been allowed access to the death-curing drugs until they had been in their "natural" seventies, bringing to the council table the probably spurious appearance of sagacity conferred by many wrinkles, an obvious physical fragility, and a sexual neutrality which was both slightly repellent and covertly enviable at the same time—a somatotype which for mankind as a whole had long ago lost its patent as the physiological stamp of hard-won wisdom, but which here among these recent immortals still exerted a queer authority, even upon Amalfi.

"If you managed to synthesize even one of the anti-agathics, you've proven yourselves better chemists than anyone else in human history," Amalfi said. "They're far and away the most complicated molecules ever found in nature; certainly we've never heard of anyone who was able to synthesize even one."

"One is all we managed to synthesize," Miramon admitted. "And the synthetic form has certain small but undesirable side-effects we've never been able to eliminate. Several others turned out to be natural sapogenins which we could raise in our artificial climate, and modify into anti-agathics by two or three subsequent fermentation steps. Finally there are four others, of very broad usefulness, which we produce by fermentation alone, using micro-organisms grown in nutrient solutions in deep tanks, into which we feed comparatively simple and cheap precursors."

"We have one like that, the first, in fact, that was ever discovered: ascomycin," Amalfi said. "I think I will stick to my original judgment. As chemists you people could obviously give all the rest of us cards and spades."

"Then it is fortunate for us, and perhaps for every sentient being everywhere, that it is not as chemists that we come seeking you," Retma said, a trifle grimly.

"Which brings me to my main question," Amalfi said. "Just why did you turn back? I can't imagine that you would have been seeking me personally, you had no reason to believe that I was anywhere within thousands of parsecs of this area; we last parted company on the other side of the home galaxy. Obviously you must have looped back toward home as soon as you were sure you had centralized control over your spindizzy installation, long before you were much past half-way to the Andromeda galaxy. What I want to know is, what turned you back?"

"There you are both right and wrong," Miramon said, with a trace of what could have been pride; it was hard to tell, for his face was extremely solemn. "We obtained reasonably close control of the anti-gravity machines only about thirty years after you and I parted company, Mayor Amalfi. When the full implications of what we had found were borne in upon us, we were highly elated. Now we had a real planet, in the radical meaning of the word, a real wanderer which could go where it chose, settling in one solar system or another and leaving it again when we so decided. By that time we were almost self-sufficient, there was obviously no need for us to become migrant workers, as your city and its enemies had been. And since we were well on the way to the second galaxy in any event, and since there seemed to be absolutely no limit to the velocities we could mount with the huge mass of our planet on which to operate, we chose to go on and explore."

"To the Andromeda galaxy?"

"Yes, and beyond. Of course we saw very little of that galaxy, which is as vast as our home; we think that it is not inhabited by any widespread, space-cruising race such as yours and mine, but in the brief sampling of its stars that we were able to take we might well simply have missed hitting upon an inhabited or colonized system. By that time, in any event, we had made the discovery which was to become the basis of our lives and purposes from then onward, and knew that we should have to return home very shortly. We left the Andromeda nebula for its satellite, the one that you identified for us as M-33 on our old star-tapestries from the Great Age, and thence took the million and a half light-year leap to the Lesser Magellanic Cloud. It was during our transition from the Lesser to the Greater Cloud that you detected us. That was, to be sure, an accident; we had intended to go directly through into the home galaxy and onward to Earth, where, our experience with you had given us good reason to believe, we might find a reservoir of knowledge great enough to cope with what we had discovered. That our own knowledge was insufficient was never for a moment in doubt.

"But it is an accident of the greatest good omen that we should have been found again by you as we were returning home, Mayor Amalfi. Surely the gods must have arranged such an accident, which otherwise is impossibly unlikely; for if there is any man not on Earth itself who can help us, you are that man."

"You were not once such a believer in the gods, as I recall," Amalfi said, smiling tightly.

"Opinions change with age; otherwise what is age for?"

"So does history," Amalfi said. "And, whether I can help you or not, it is a lucky accident that you stopped here before carrying on into the home lens. Earth is no longer dominant there. We've had considerable difficulty in understanding what actually is going on, the messages that we get from there come pouring in to us in such an enormous garble; but of one thing I'm sure: there's a huge new imperialism on the rise there, on its way to becoming as powerful as Earth once was, and as Vega was before Earth. It calls itself the Web of Hercules, and what remains of Earth's interstellar empire doesn't appear to be putting up much of a resistance against it. If you want my advice, I would suggest that you stay out of the home galaxy entirely, or you may well be gobbled down whole."

There was a long silence around the Hevian council table. At last, Miramon said:

"This leaves us with little recourse indeed. It may well be that there is no answer, as we have often suspected. Or it may be that the gods have indeed brought us back to the one source of wisdom that we need."

"We will know soon enough," Retma said quietly. "If in that instant there will be time enough to know anything. Or enough of time left thereafter to remember it."

"I shall probably be unable to advise you so long as I don't know what you're talking about," Amalfi said, impressed in spite of himself by the tone of high seriousness with which the Hevians spoke. "Just what was the discovery that turned you back? What is the forthcoming event that you seem to dread?"

"Nothing less," Retma said evenly, "than the imminent coming to an end of time itself."

For a while, even after they had explained it to him, Amalfi was so unable to believe that the Hevians had meant what they said that he was prepared to dismiss it as one of those superstitions with which He had been riddled, like many another provincial planet, when the Okies had first made contact with it. That time must have a stop was a proposition that nothing in all his long life had prepared him to accept even for an instant. Even after it became reluctantly clear to him that what Miramon and the Hevians had found in the intergalactic deeps had been a real event with real implications, and one which Amalfi's own people—particularly Schloss' group—were prepared to document, event and implication alike, he continued to be unable to do more with it than dismiss it out of hand.

He said so, at a conference on shipboard which included Miramon, Retma, Dr. Schloss, Carrel, and—by Dirac—Jake and Dr. Gifford Bonner, the latter the leader of that group of New Earth philosophers which Hazleton had recently joined, called the Stochastics. "If what you say is true," he said, "there's nothing to be done about it anyhow. Time will come to an end, and that's that. But the end of the world has been predicted often before, I seem to remember from history, and here we all are still; I can't credit that so vast a process as the whole physical universe could possibly come to an end in the flicker of an eyelash, and since I can't believe it, I'm not suddenly going to start behaving as if I did. No more do I see why anyone else should."

"Amalfi, you're quite right! You don't understand," Dr. Schloss said. "Of course the end of the universe has been predicted often before. It's one of those two-pronged choices that any philosopher has to make: either you hold that the universe will at some time come to an end, or else you arrive at the position that it never can; there are intermediate guesses that you can make, that's where we get our cyclical theories, but essentially they're simply hedges. If you decide that the universe has a limited lifetime, then you must begin to think about when that life will come to an end, on the basis of whatever data are available to you. We have been agreed for millennia that the universe cannot last for ever, however we've hedged the agreement, so that leaves us nothing to quarrel about but the date at which we fix the end. And sooner or later, too, the time was going to come when we had enough data to fix even the date without doubt. The Hevians have brought us sufficient facts to do that now; the date is fixed, whatever it proves to be, without cavil or quibble. If we are to talk about the matter intelligently at all, there is a fixed fact with which we must begin. It is not open to argument. It is a fact."

"I think", Amalfi said in a voice of steel, "that you have all gone quietly insane. You should listen to the City Fathers for a while on this subject, as I have; if you like, I can give you a Dirac line to them from right here aboard ship, and you can hear some of the memories that they have stored up—some of them dating back long before spaceflight; our city is very old. You should hear particularly the stories about the end of the world which emerge as inevitably as a plant from a seed every time someone takes it into his head to believe that he has a direct wire to the Almighty. Some of the stories, of course, are just jokes, like the many predictions of the end of the world which were made by a man named Voliva, who *knew* that the Earth was flat; or the predictions of Armageddon that came repeatedly from an Earthly sect called the Believers, which was riding high on Earth during the very decade when both the spindizzy and the anti-agathics were discovered. But high intelligence doesn't prevent you from falling into this kind of apocryphal madness, either; seven centuries before spaceflight on Earth, the greatest scientist of that time, a man named Bacon, was predicting the imminent arrival of Anti-Christ simply because he was unable to persuade his contemporaries to adopt scientific method, which he had just invented. Furthermore, I may add, in the decade just before spaceflight on Earth, all the best minds of the age saw no future for the human race, and all other air-breathing life on Earth, but complete obliteration in a world-wide thermonuclear war, which over a period of eight years could have broken out within any given twenty-minute period. And in that, Dr. Schloss, they were quite right; their world really could have ended during any one of these twenty-minute periods; the physical possibilities were there, but somehow the world managed to last until spaceflight, and then the end of the world became only a spectre, burned out by starlight, as the ghosts of night-bound peoples evaporate from their mythologies as soon as they're able to produce light even at midnight simply by tripping a switch."

He looked around at the faces of the men drawn up at the ship's chart table. Few of them would meet his eyes; most of them were looking down at the table itself, or at their own hands. Their expressions were those of men who had been listening to a mass murderer attempting to enter a plea of insanity.

"Amalfi," Jake's voice said abruptly from the Dirac, "the time for forensics is past. This question does not have two sides, except for the right side and the wrong side, and we are going to have to shuck you off as a brilliant advocate for the wrong side. You have done your magnificent best, but since the right side does not need an advocate, you have been wasting your breath. Let me ask the rest of this conference: What shall we do now? Does it appear that, as the Hevians think, there is anything at all that we can do? I am inclined to doubt it."

"So am I," Dr. Schloss said, though there was nothing in his manner to suggest the gloom inherent in his conclusion; he seemed rather to be as intensely interested as Amalfi had ever seen him in his life. "For temporal creatures to hope to survive the end of time is surely as futile as a fish hoping to survive being thrown into a sun. The paradox is immediate, on the surface, and quite inescapable."

"No technical problem is ever that insoluble," Amalfi said in exasperation. "Miramon, if you will pardon me for passing such a judgment—and I don't care if you don't—I think you are suffering from the same syndrome as Dr. Freeman and Dr. Schloss: you have grown old before your time. You've lost your sense of adventure."

"Not entirely," Miramon said, regarding Amalfi with an expression of grave and hurt disappointment. "We, at least, are not yet convinced that there is no answer; if we do not find it here, we have every intention of continuing to travel in the hope of finding someone with whom we can combine forces, someone who may have some solution to suggest. If we find no one, then we shall continue to seek that solution ourselves."

"Good for you," Amalfi said fiercely. "And by God I'll go with you. We can't very well re-enter our own galaxy, but the next one is NGC 6822, that's about a million lightyears from here—for you, that's only a hop. And at least we'd be in motion; we wouldn't be sitting around here with folded hands waiting for the blow to fall."

"That would be motion without purpose," Miramon

said solemnly. "I agree with you that it would be dangerous and unwise to risk any entanglement with the Web of Hercules, whatever that may be; but I can see no better point in cruising from one galaxy to another solely in the bare hope of encountering a high civilization which might be able to help us, and all the rest of the universe with us. We have that hope, but it cannot be the final goal of our journey: our ultimate destination must be the centre of the metagalaxy, the hub of all the galaxies of space-time. It is only there, where all the forces of the universe lie in dynamic balance, that anyone can hope to take any action to escape or to modify the end which is coming. There is, after all, not much time left before that moment is due. And above all, Mayor Amalfi, it is not simply a technical problem; it is an ending which was written organically into the fundamental structure of the universe itself, written in the beginning by what hands we know not; all that we can know now is that it was foreordained."

And from this conclusion, though Amalfi's own psyche had been fighting against its acceptance since the moment that he himself had realized it was so, there was really no escape. Conceptually, the universe had been a reasonably comfortable place to live in, in primitive atomic theory, which offered the assurance that everything, earth, air, fire or water, steel and oranges, man or star, was ultimately composed of submicroscopic vortices called protons and electrons, leavened a little with neutrons and neutrinos which had no charge, and bound together by a disorderly but homely family of mesons. The type case was the hydrogen atom, one proton sitting cosily on the hearth, contentedly positive in charge, while about it wove one electron, surrounded by its negative field like crackling cat's fur. That was the simple case; but one was assured that even in the heaviest and most complicated atoms, even those man-made ones like plutonium, one need only add more and heavier logs to the fire, and more cats would come droning about it; it would be hard to tell one cat from another, but this is the customary penalty the owner of hundreds pays.

The first omen that there was something wrong with this chromo of sub-microscopic and universal domesticity appeared, as all good omens should, in the skies. Back on Earth, nearly half a century before spaceflight, some astronomer whose name is quite lost had noticed that two or three of the millions of meteors that entered Earth's atmosphere every day exploded at a height and with a violence which could not be accounted for by an eccentricity of orbit or velocity; and in one of those great flights of fancy which account in the long run for every new link in the great chain of understanding, he had a dream of something which he called "contraterrene" matter—a matter made of fire with cat's fur, which would be circled by cats in flames: matter in which the fundamental hydrogen atom would have a nucleus which would be an anti-proton, with the mass of a proton but carrying a negative charge, around which would orbit an anti-electron, with the negligible mass of an electron, but carrying a positive charge. A meteor of atoms constructed on this model, he reasoned, would explode with especial violence at the first contact with even the faintest traces of Earth's normal-matter atmosphere; and such meteors would suggest that somewhere in the universe there were whole planets, whole suns, whole galaxies composed of such matter, whose barest touch would be more than death—would be ultimate and complete annihilation, each form of matter converting the other wholly into energy in a flaming and total embrace.

Curiously, the contra-terrene meteors died out of the theory shortly thereafter, while the theory itself survived. The exploding meteors were found to be easier to explain in more conventional terms, but anti-matter survived, and by the middle of the twentieth century experimental physicists were even able to produce the stuff a few atoms at a time. Those topsy-turvy atoms proved to be non-viable beyond a few millionths of a micro-second, and it gradually became clear that even in this short lifetime the time in which they lived was running backwards. The particles of which they were made were born, in the great clumsy bevatrons of that age, some micro-seconds in the future, and their assembly into atoms of anti-matter in the present time of the observers was in fact the moment of their death. Obviously anti-matter was not only theoretically possible, but could exist; and it could not exist in this universe in any assemblage so gross as a meteor; if there were worlds and galaxies made of anti-matter, they existed only in some unthinkable separate continuum where time and the entropy gradient ran backwards. Such a continuum would require at least four extra dimensions in addition to the conventional four of experience.

As the universe of normal matter expanded, unwound and ran down toward its inevitable heat-death, somewhere near by and yet in a "somewhere" unimaginable by man, a duplicate universe as vast and complex was contracting, winding up, approaching the supernal concentration of mass and energy called the monobloc. As complete dispersion, darkness and silence was to be the fate of the universe in which the arrow of time pointed down the entropy gradient, so in the anti-matter universe the end was to be mass beyond mass, energy beyond energy, raw glare and fury to the ultimate power raging in a primeval "atom" no bigger across than the orbit of Saturn. And out of one universe might come the other; in the universe of normal matter the monobloc was the beginning, but in the universe of anti-matter it would be the end; in a universe of normal entropy, the monobloc is intolerable and must explode; in a universe of negative entropy, the heat-death is intolerable and must condense. In either case, the command is: *Let there be light.*

What the visible, tangible universe had been like before the monobloc was, however, agreed to be for ever unknowable. The classic statement had been made many centuries earlier by St. Augustine, who, when asked what God might have been doing before He created the universe, replied that He was constructing a hell for persons who asked such questions; thus "pre-Augustinean time" came to be something that a historian could know all about, but a physicist, by definition, nothing.

Until now; for if the Hevians were right, they had lifted that curtain a little way and caught an instant's glimpse of the unknowable.

To have looked it full in the face could have been no more fatal.

During the course of their exultant drive upon the

Andromeda galaxy, the Hevians had discovered that one of their spindizzies—oddly, it was one of the machines which had been new-built for the project, not one of the old and somewhat abused drivers which had been dismounted from the Okie city—was beginning to run somewhat hot. This was a problem which was then brand new to them, and rather than take chances on the to them unknown effects which might be produced by such a machine were it to run really wild, they shut down their entire spindizzy network while repairs were made, leaving behind only a 0·02 per cent screen necessary to protect the planet's atmosphere and heat budget.

And it was then and there, in the utter silences of intergalactic space, that their instruments detected for the first time in human history the whispers of continuous creation: the tiny *ping* of new atoms of hydrogen being born, one by one, out of nothing at all.

This would alone and in itself have been a sobering enough experience for any man of a thoughtful cast of mind, even one who lacked the Hevians' history of preoccupation with religious questions; no one could view the birth of the raw material from which the whole known universe was built, out of what was demonstrably nothingness, without being shaken by the conviction that there must also be a Creator, and that He must be in the immediate vicinity of where His work was proceeding. Those tiny pings and pips in the Hevians' instruments seemed at first to leave no room left in the long arguments of cosmogony and cosmology for any cyclical theory of the universe, any continuous and eternal systole/diastole from monobloc to heat-death and back again, with a Creator required only at the remote inception of the rhythmic process, or not at all. Here was creation in process: the invisible Finger touched nothingness, and from nothing came something; the ultimate absurdity, which, because it was ultimate, could be nothing else but divine.

Yet the Hevians were sophisticated enough to be suspicious. Historically, fundamental discoveries were dependably ambiguous; this discovery, which on the face of it seemed to provide a flat answer to 25,000 years of theological speculation, and in effect to bring God into inarguable being for the first time since He had been postulated by some Stone Age sun-worshipper or mushroom-eating mystic, could not be as simple as it seemed. It had been won too easily; too much else is implied by the continual creating existence of a present God to make it tenable that that existence should be provable by so simple and single a physical datum, arrived at by what could honestly only be described as ordinary accident.

Gifford Bonner was later to remark that it had been fortunate beyond belief that it had been the Hevians, a people only recently winning back to some degree of scientific sophistication, but which had never lost its sense of the continuity and the overwhelming complexity of theology in a scientific age, who had first been allowed to hear these tiny birth-cries in the nursery of time. The typical Earthman of the end of the Third Millennium, with his engineer's bias, philosophically wedded in about equal measure to a sentimentally hard-headed "common sense" and a raw and naive mystique of Progress (it was at about this point in Bonner's analysis that Amalfi had felt a slight impulse to squirm), might easily have taken the datum at face value and walked the plank on it directly into a morass of telepathy, the racial unconscious, personal reincarnation or any of a hundred other traps which await the scientifically oriented man who does not know that he too is as thorough-going a mystic as a fakir lying on a bed of nails.

The Hevians were suspicious; they questioned the discovery first of all only on the subject of what it said it was saying. Theology could wait. If continuous creation was a fact, then primarily that ruled out that there should ever have been a monobloc in the history of the universe, or that there should ever be a heat-death; instead, it would always go along like this, world without end. Therefore, if the discovery was as fundamentally ambiguous as all such discoveries before had proven to be, it should in the same breath be implying exactly the opposite; ask it *that* question, and see what it says.

This singularly tough-minded approach paid off at once, though the further implications which it offered for inspection proved in no way easier to digest than the first and contrary set had been. Taking a long chance with the still largely unfamiliar machines, and with the precarious life of their entire planet, the Hevians shut down their spindizzies entirely and listened more intently.

In that utmost of dead silences, the upsetting whisper of continuous creation proved to have two voices. Each pinging birth-pang was not a single note, but a duo. As each atom of hydrogen leapt into being from nowhere into the universe of experience, a sinister twin, a hydrogen atom of anti-matter, came there in that instant to die, from . . . somewhere else.

And there it was. Even what had seemed to be fundamental, ineluctable proof of one-way time and continuous creation could also be regarded as inarguable evidence for a cyclical cosmology. In a way, to the Hevians, it was satisfying; this was physics as they knew it to be, an idiot standing at a cross-roads shouting "God went thataway!" and managing to point down all four roads at once. Nevertheless, it left them a legacy of dread. This single many-barbed burr of a datum, which could have been obtained under no other circumstances, was also sufficient in itself to endorse the existence of an entire second universe of anti-matter, congruent point for point with the universe of experience of normal matter, but opposite to it in sign. What appeared to have been the birth of a hydrogen atom of anti-matter, simultaneous with the birth of the normal hydrogen atom, was actually its death; there was now no doubt that time ran backwards in the anti-matter universe, and so did the entropy gradient, one being demonstrably a function of the other.

The concept, of course, was old—so old, in fact, that Amalfi had difficulty in remembering just when in his lifetime it had become so familiar to him that he had forgotten about it entirely. Its revival here by the Hevians struck him at first as an exasperating anachronism, calculated only to get in the way of the real work of practical men. He was in particular rather scornful of the notion of a universe in which negative entropy could be an operating principle; under such circumstances, his rustily squeaking memory pointed out, cause and effect would not preserve even the rough statistical associations which they were allowed in the universe of experience; energy would accumulate, events would undo themselves, water would run uphill, old men would clump into existence out of the air and soil and unlearn their profitless ways back toward their mothers' wombs.

"Which is what they do in any event," Gifford Bonner had said gently. "But actually, I doubt that it's that paradoxical, Amalfi. Both of these universes can be regarded as unwinding, as running down, as losing energy with each transaction. The fact that from our point of view the anti-matter universe seems to be gaining energy is simply a bias built into the way we're forced to look at things. Actually these two universes probably are simply unwinding in opposite directions, like two millstones. Though the two arrows of time seem to be pointing in opposite directions, they probably both point downhill, like fingerboards at the crest of a single road. If the dynamics of it bother you, bear in mind that both are four-dimensional *continua* and from that point of view both are wholly static."

"Which brings us to the crucial question of contiguity," Jake said cheerfully. "The point is, these two four-dimensional *continua* are intimately related, as the twin events the Hevians observed make very plain; which I suppose must mean that we must allow for a total of at least sixteen dimensions to contain the whole system. Which is no particular surprise in itself; you need at least that many to accommodate the atomic nucleus of average complexity comfortably. What is surprising is that the two *continua* are approaching each other; I agree with Miramon that the observations his people made can't be interpreted any other way; up to now, the fact that gravitation in the two universes is also opposite in sign seems to have kept them apart, but that repulsion or pressure or whatever you want to call it is obviously growing steadily weaker. Somewhere in the future, the near future, it will decline to zero, there will be a Pythagorean point-for-point collision between the two universes as a whole——"

"—and it's hard to imagine how any physical framework, even one that allows sixteen dimensions of elbow-room, will be able to contain the energy that's going to be released," Dr. Schloss said. "The monobloc isn't even in the running; if it ever existed, it was just a wet firecracker by comparison."

"Translation: *blooey*," Carrel said.

"It's perfectly possible that a rational cosmology is going to have to accommodate all three events," Gifford Bonner said. "I mean by that the monobloc, the heat-death, and this thing—this event that seems to fall midway between the two. Curious; there are a number of myths, and ancient philosophical systems, that allow for such a break or discontinuity right in the middle of the span of existence; Giordano Bruno, Earth's first relativist, called it the period of Inter-destruction, and a compatriot of his named Vico allowed for it in what was probably the first cyclical theory of ordinary human history; and in Scandinavian mythology it was called the Ginnunga-Gap. But I wonder, Dr. Schloss, if the destruction is going to be quite as total as you suggest. I am nobody's physicist, I freely confess, but it seems to me that if these two universes are opposite in sign *at every point*, as everyone at this meeting has been implying, then the result cannot be *only* a general transformation of the matter on both sides into energy. There will be energy transformed into matter, too, on just as large a scale, after which the gravitational pressure should begin to build up again and the two universes, having in effect passed through each other and exchanged hats, will begin retreating from each other once more. Or have I missed something crucial?"

"I'm not sure that the argument is as elegant as it appears on the surface," Retma said. "That awaits Dr. Schloss's mathematical analysis, of course; but in the meantime I cannot help but wonder why, for instance, if this simultaneous creation-interdestruction-destruction cycle is truly cyclical, it should have this ornamental waterspout of continuous creation attached to it? A machinery of creation which involves no less than three universal cataclysms in each cycle should not need to be powered by a sort of continuous drip; either the one is too grandiose, or the other is insufficient. Besides, continuous creation implies a steady state, which is irreconcilable."

"I don't know about that," Jake said. "It doesn't sound like anything the Milne transformations couldn't handle; it's probably just a clock function."

"Defined, as I recall, as a mathematical expression about the size of a bottle of aspirin," Carrel said ruefully.

"Well, there's one thing I'm perfectly certain of", Amalfi growled, "and that is that it's damned unlikely anybody is going to be around to care about the exact results of the collision after it happens. At least not at the rate this hassel is going. Is there actually anything useful that we can do, or would we be better off spending all this time playing poker?"

"That", Miramon said, "is exactly what we know

least about. In fact it would appear that we know nothing about it whatsoever."

"Mr. Miramon——" Web Hazleton's voice spoke from the shadows and stopped. Obviously he was waiting to be told that he was breaking his promise not to interrupt, but it was as plain to Amalfi as it was to the rest of the group that he was interrupting nothing now; his voice had broken only a dead and despairing silence.

"Go ahead, Web," Amalfi said.

"Well, I was just thinking. Mr. Miramon came here looking for somebody to help him do something he doesn't know how to do himself. Now he thinks we don't know how to do it either. But what was it?"

"He's just said that he doesn't know," Amalfi said gently.

"That isn't what I mean," Web said hesitantly. "What I mean is, what would he *like* to do, even if he doesn't know how to do it? Even if it's impossible?"

Bonner's voice chuckled softly in the still shipboard air. "That's right," he said, "the ends determine the means. A hen is only an egg's device for producing another egg. Is that Hazleton's grandson? Good for you, Web."

"There are a good many experiments that ought to be performed, if only we knew how to design them," Miramon admitted thoughtfully. "First of all, we ought to have a better date for the catastrophe than we have now, 'the near future' is a huge block of time under these conditions, almost as shapeless a target as 'sometime'; we would need it defined to the millisecond just to begin with. I applaud the young Earthman's brilliant common sense, but I refuse to delude myself by asking for more than that; even that seems hopeless."

"Why?" Amalfi said. "What would you need to calculate it from? Given the data, the City Fathers can handle the calculations; they were designed to handle any mathematical operation once the parameters were filled, and in a thousand years I've never known them to fail to come through on that kind of thing, usually within two or three minutes; never as long as a day."

"I remember your City Fathers," Miramon said, with a brief ironical motion of his eyebrows which was perhaps a last vestigial tremor of his old savage awe at the things which were the city and of the city. "But the major parameter that needs to be filled here is a precise determination of the energy level of the other universe."

"Why, that shouldn't be so very difficult," Dr. Schloss said, in dawning astonishment. "That can't be anything but a transform of the energy level in our own universe; the mayor's right, the City Fathers could give you that almost before you could finish stating the problem to them; t-tau transforms are the fundamental stuff of faster-than-light space travel—I'm astonished that you've been able to get along without them."

"Not so," Jake said. "No doubt the t-tau relationships are congruent on both sides of the barrier, I don't doubt that for a minute, but you're dealing in sixteen dimensions here; along what axis are you going to impose the congruency? Are you going to assume that t-time and tau-time apply uniformly and transformably along all sixteen axes? You can't do that, unless you're willing to involve the total system in such a double, which in t-time involves a monobloc for the whole apparatus; that's hopeless. At least it's hopeless for us, in the time we have left; we'd be frittering away our days in chase of endlessly retreating decimals. You might just as well set the City Fathers to work giving you a final figure for *pi*."

"I stand corrected," Dr. Schloss said, his tone halfway between wry humour and stiff embarrassment. "You're quite right, Miramon; there's a discontinuity here which we can't read from theory. How inelegant."

"Elegance can wait," Amalfi said. "In the meantime, why is it so impossible to get an energy-level reading from the other side? Dr. Schloss, your research group used to talk about their hopes of constructing an anti-matter artifact. Couldn't we use such a thing as an exploratory missile to the other side?"

"No," Dr. Schloss said promptly. "You forget that such an object wouldn't be on the other side—it would be on our side. We would have to work out some way of assembling it in the future of the experiment; by the time we were first able to see it, in the present of the experiment, it would be in an advanced state of decay, to say the least, and would then evolve only to the condition in which we assembled it. No reading that we got from it would tell us anything but how anti-matter behaves in our universe; it would tell us nothing about any universe in which anti-matter is normal."

After a moment, he added thoughtfully: "And besides, that would be a project hard to realize in anything under a century. I'd be more inclined to say it would take two; under the circumstances I too would rather be playing poker."

"Well, I wouldn't," Jake said unexpectedly. "I think Amalfi may be right in principle. Difficult though the problem is, there ought to be some sort of probe that we could extend across the discontinuity. Mind you, I agree that the anti-matter artifact is the wrong approach entirely; the thing would have to be absolutely immaterial, a construct made entirely out of what we could pick up in no-man's-land. But seeing across long distances under great odds is the discipline I was trained in. I don't think we should count this an impossible problem. Schloss, how do you feel about this? If you and your group are willing to give up your anti-matter artifact for poker, would you be willing to work with me on this a while? I'll need your background, but you'll need my point of view; between us we just might devise the instrument and get the message. Mind you, Miramon, I hold out no hope, but——"

"—except the hope you hold out," Miramon said, his eyes shining. "Now I am hearing from you what I hoped to hear. This is the voice of the Earth of memory. We will give you everything you need that is within our power to give; we give you our planet, to begin with; but the universe, the twin universes, the unthinkable meta-universe you must take for yourselves. We remember you now; you have always had that boundless ambition." His voice darkened suddenly. "And we shall be your disciples; that, too, is as it has always been. Only begin; that is all we ask."

Amalfi gathered the consensus of the present eyes around the chart table. Such agreement as he needed from the listeners on New Earth he was able to gather almost as well from the silence.

"I think", he said slowly, "that we have begun already."

4

FABR-SUITHE

It was hot on the Hevian hillside in the post-noon glare of the great Cepheid about which the planet was now orbiting at the respectful distance of thirty-five astronomical units—thirty-five times the distance of old Earth from the Sun. At this distance the star, which had a mean absolute magnitude of plus one, was barely tolerable at the peak of its eight-day cycle; at the bottom of the cycle, when the star's radiation had dropped by a factor of 25, it got cold enough on He to nip one's ears—far from an ideal situation for a predominantly agricultural planet, but the Hevians did not expect to remain in the vicinity for as long as one growing season.

Web and Estelle lay in the long grass of the hillside under the hot regard of that swollen star and slowly got their breaths back. Web in particular was glad for the recess. The morning had begun in sober exploration of Fabr-Suithe, He's greatest monument to its own past, and He's present centre of pure philosophy; thus far it was the only place they had found on He which they were allowed to explore by themselves, by both the adult Hevians and their own people. This morning, however, this freedom had had an unexpected but logical consequence: they had found that Fabr-Suithe was also one of the few cities on He where Hevian children were free to roam. Elsewhere there were far too many machines vital to the life of the planet as a whole; the Hevians could not afford the chance that children might get into the works, nor, with their sparse population, could they afford the loss of even a single life.

Web and Estelle had changed into the chiton-like Hevian costume the moment they had been told that they would be allowed to explore the city, albeit in very limited terms, but it did not take the Hevian youngsters long to penetrate this disguise, since Web and Estelle spoke their language only in a most rudimentary way. This language block was in part a nuisance—for although most adult Hevians spoke the mixture of English, Interlingua and Russian which was the *beche-le-mer* of deep spacc, learned long ago from the Okies, none of the children did—but it was also a blessing, since it precluded any extensive interrogation of Web and Estelle about their own world, culture and background. Shortly, instead, they found themselves involved in an elaborate chase game called Matrix, rather like run-sheep-run combined with chequers—except that it was three-dimensional, for it was played in a twelve-story building with transparent floors so that one could always see the positions of the other players, and with strategically placed spindizzy and friction-field shafts for fast transit from one floor to another. Web was the first to develop the suspicion that the building had either been designed for the game or had been totally abandoned to it, for the transparent floors were appropriately ruled, and the structure otherwise did not seem to contain anything or to be used for any other purpose.

Web had found the game itself exhilarating at first, but rather baffling too, and he was generally the first player to be eliminated. Had it not been for an impromptu change in the rules, he would have been It in nearly every new round, and even under the aegis of the new rules he did not make a very brave showing. Estelle, on the other hand, took to Matrix as though she had been born in the game, and within half an hour her lanky-legged, slender figure, as bosomless and hipless as any of the boys', was darting in and out of the kaleidoscope of running figures with inordinate grace and swiftness. When time was called for lunch, Web's labouring lungs and bruised ego more than welcomed the chance to escape from the city entirely for the hot stillness of the fallow hills.

"They're nice; I like them," Estelle said, rising to one elbow to attack, meditatively, a gourd-shaped green and silver melon which one of the Hevian boys had given her, apparently as a prize. At the first bite, there was a low but prolonged hiss, and the air around them became impregnated with a fragrance so overwhelmingly spicy that Estelle had to sneeze five times in quick succession. Web began to laugh, but the laughter ended abruptly in a paroxysmal sneeze of his own.

"They *love* us," he said, wiping his eyes. "You're so good at their game, they've given you a sneeze-gas bomb to keep you from playing it any longer."

The odour diminished gradually, carried off by what little breeze there was. After a while Estelle cautiously put two thumbs into the wound she had made and broke the melon open. Nothing else happened; the odour was now tolerable, and then abruptly became both barely detectable and overpoweringly mouth-watering. Estelle handed him half. He bit into the crisp white pulp more deeply than he had intended. The result made him close his eyes; it tasted like quick-frozen music.

They finished it in reverent silence and, wiping their mouths on their chitons, lay back. After a while, Estelle said:

"I wish we could talk to them better."

"Miramon can talk to *us* well enough," Web said somnolently. "He didn't have to learn our language the hard way, either. They do it here by machine, like we used to do it when we were Okies. I wish we still did it that way."

"Hypnopaedia?" Estelle said. "But I thought that was all dead and done for. You didn't really *learn* anything that way; just facts."

"That's right, just facts. It didn't teach you to relate. For that you have to have a tutor. But it was good for learning things like 1 × 1 = 10, or the tables in the back of the book, or the 850 words you most need to know in a new language. It used to take only five hundred hours to cram all that stuff into you, by EEG feedback, flicker, oral repetition, and I don't know what all else—and the whole time, you were under hypnosis."

"It sounds too easy," Estelle said sleepily.

"The easy parts of things ought to be easy," Web said. "What's the point of having to learn them by rote? That takes too much time. You know yourself that something you can learn in ten repetitions, or five, it takes some kids thirty repetitions to learn. So you have to sit around through twenty or twenty-five repetitions that you don't need. If there's anything I hate about school, it's drill—all that time wasted that you could actually be doing something with."

Suddenly Web became conscious of a peculiar flopping sound at the crest of the hill behind him. He knew well enough that there were no dangerous animals left on He, but he realized that he had been hearing the sound for some time while he was talking; and the notion occurred to him that his definition of a dangerous animal might not necessarily make a good match with that of a Hevian. Anyhow, he could hope; he could use a tiger to best, along about now. He twisted quickly to his hands and knees.

"Don't be silly," Estelle said, without moving or even opening her eyes. "It's only Ernest."

The svengali appeared over the crest of the hill and came humping itself through the tall grass in a symphony of desperate disorganization. It gave Web only the briefest of glances; and then bent upon Estelle the reproachful stare of an animal utterly betrayed, but still—it hoped you noticed—firm in the true faith. Web stifled his impulse to laugh, for in fact he could hardly blame the poor creature; since it was as brainless as it was sexless—despite its name—it had been able to contrive no better way of keeping up with Estelle than to follow her through her every move in the Matrix game, a discipline for which it was so magnificently unequipped that it had only just now finished. It was lucky that the children had not counted it as a player, or poor Ernest would have been It to—Web thought with unfocused uneasiness—the end of time.

"We could sign up for it here," Web said abruptly.

"For what? Hypnopaedia? Your grandmother wouldn't let us."

Web turned around and sat up, plucking a long hollow blade of the bamboo-like grass and sinking his grinding teeth thoughtfully into the woody butt-end. "But she isn't here," he said.

"No, but she will be," Estelle said. "And she's a school officer on New Earth. I used to hear her fighting about it with my father when I was a child. She used to tell him he was out of his mind. She would say: 'Why do kids need all this calculus and history now? What good is it to somebody who's going to have to go out and hoe a virgin planet?' She used to make poor Dad stutter something awful."

"But she isn't here," Web repeated, with a little unwilling exasperation. He had just realized that Estelle's face with its closed eyes, so perfectly in repose in the blue-white light of this one-day-long summer, was lovelier than anything he had ever seen before. He found that he could not go on.

At the same moment, the svengali felt rested enough to take a concensus among the scattered ganglia which served it, however badly, for a brain, and concluded that its long soulful stare at Estelle was doing it no good at all. Simultaneously one of its limbs, which had the whole time been inching in the direction of one of the melon rinds, suddenly passed a threshold and telegraphed back to the rest of the animal the implications of that now faint spicy odour. All the rest of Ernest flowed eagerly into that arm and bunched itself around the rind; and then the polyp was rolling helplessly down the hill, curled into a ball, with the melon rind clutched firmly in the middle. As it rolled, it emitted a small thrilling whistle of alarm which made Web's back hairs stir—it was the first time he had ever heard a svengali make a sound—but it would not let go of its prize; it came to rest in the middle of a rivulet in the valley, and was washed gently downstream out of sight, still faintly protesting and avidly digesting.

"There goes Ernest," Web said.

"I know. I heard him. He's such a stupid. But he'll be back. Your grandmother will be here too. Once the Mayor and Miramon and Dr. Schloss and the rest decided to stay on He, because of all the work they have to do here, they had to send home for somebody to take care of us. They don't think we can take care of ourselves. They wouldn't let us go knocking all around a strange planet all by ourselves."

"Maybe not," Web said reluctantly. He tested the proposition; it seemed to hold water. "But why would it have to be grandmother?"

"Well, it wouldn't be Daddy, because he has to stay on New Earth and work on the New Earth part of the problem that we're working on here," Estelle said. "And it wouldn't be your grandfather because he has to stay home on New Earth and be mayor while Mayor Amalfi's here. It wouldn't be my mother because they're not scientists or philosophers and would just clutter up He even more than we're doing. If they're going to fly anyone out here to oversee us, it has to be your grandmother."

"I suppose so," Web said. "That'll put a crimp in us, for sure."

"It'll do more than that," Estelle said tranquilly. "She'll send us home."

"She wouldn't do that!"

"Yes she would. That's the way they think. She'll be practical about it."

"That's not being practical," Web protested. "It's treachery, that's what it is. She can't come all the way here to take care of us on He, just as an excuse to take us off He."

Estelle did not reply. After a moment Web opened his eyes, belatedly realizing that a shadow had fallen across his face. The Hevian boy who had given Estelle the melon was standing above them, deferentially, respecting their silence, but obviously poised to renew the game when they were ready. Behind him, the heads of the other Hevian children bobbed over the hill, obviously wondering what the strangers and their boneless, odd-smelling pet would do next, but leaving the initiative to their spokesman.

"Hello," Estelle said, sitting up again.

"Hello," the tall boy said hesitantly. "Yes?"

For a moment he seemed baffled; then, making the best of the situation, he sat down and went on in as simple a Hevian as he could contrive.

"You are rested. Yes? Shall we play another game?"

"No more for me," Web said, almost indignantly. "Then play Matrix yesterday, tomorrow sometime day. Yes?"

"No, no," the Hevian boy said. "Not Matrix. This is another game, a resting game. You play it sitting down. We call it the lying game."

"Oh. How works it?"

"Everyone takes turns. Each tells a story. It must be a real story, without any truth in it. The other players are the jury. You gain a point for everything in the story that is clearly true. The low score wins."

"I lost about five key words in there somewhere," Estelle said to Web. "How does it go again?"

Web explained quickly. Although his spoken command of the Hevian language was limited to the tenses of past indictable, present excitable and future irredeemable, his vocabulary a thoroughly unbotanical mixture of stems and roots, and his declensions one massive disinclination to decline, he found that he was developing a fair facility at understanding the language, at least when it was being spoken this slowly. It was quite probable that he too had lost five words in the course of the Hevian boy's speech, but he had picked up their meaning from context; Estelle apparently was still trying to translate word by word, instead of striving first to catch the total import of the sentence.

"Oh, I see," Estelle said. "But how do they rate one truth over another? If in my story the sun rises in the morning, and I also say I'm wearing this whatever-it-is, this chiton, do I get docked one point for each?"

"I'll try to ask," Web said doubtfully. "I'm not sure I have all the nouns I need."

He put the question to the Hevian boy, finding it necessary to be rather more abstract than he wished; but the boy grasped not only the sense of what he was trying to say, but worked his way back to the concrete nouns with impressive insight.

"The jury will decide," the boy said. "But there are rules. A dress is only a little truth, and costs only one point. Sunrise on a captive planet, like New Earth, is a natural law, that may cost you fifty. On a free planet like He, it may be only partly true and cost you ten. Or it may be a flat lie and cost you nothing. That is why we have the jury."

Web had to have this restated to him in increasingly simpler terms before he chanced explaining it in turn to Estelle; but at last he was reasonably sure that both the New Earth players understood the rules of the game. To make assurance doubly sure, he asked the Hevians to begin, so that he and Estelle could become familiar with the kinds of lies which were most admired, and the way the jury of players penalized each inadvertent truth.

The first two stories came close to convincing him that he was being overcautious. At the very least it seemed plain, both from the terms in which the game had been described and the stories as they were told, that the Hevians as a race had little talent for fiction. The third player, however, a girl of about nine who obviously had been bursting with impatience for her turn to come around, stunned him completely. The moment she was called upon, she began:

"This morning I saw a letter, and the address on it was Four. The letter had feet, and the feet had shoes on them. It was delivered by missile, but it walked all the way. Though it is Four for four, it's triple treble trouble," she wound up triumphantly.

There was a short, embarrassed silence.

"That doesn't sound like a lie at all," Estelle said to Web, relapsing into her own language. "It sounds more like a riddle."

"That was not fair," the Hevian leader was telling the nine-year-old at the same time in a stern voice. "We hadn't explained the rules of the coup." He turned to Web and Estelle. "Another part of the game is to try to tell a story which is entirely true, but sounds like a lie. In the coup, the jury penalizes you for lying if it can catch you. If you aren't caught, you have told a perfect truth, which wins the round even over a perfect lie. But it was unfair of Pyla to try for a coup before we'd explained it to you."

"I challenge once," Web said grayly. "Is really this morning was? If, then we had had knowed; but we haven't."

"This morning," Pyla insisted, determinedly defending her coup in the face of the group's obvious disapproval. "You weren't there then. I saw you leave."

"How do you know about all these?" Web said.

"I hung around," the girl said. Abruptly, she giggled. "And I heard you two talking, too, behind the hill."

Since the whole of her answer was offered in a fluent, though heavily accented Okie *beche-le-mer*, there were obviously no further questions to be asked.

Web was feeling just barely civil toward females, but he offered Pyla his politest smile. "In that case," he said formally, "you win. We thank you from our heartmost bottom. This is good news."

He never did quite make up his mind whether his imperfect knowledge of Hevian made this polite speech come out as "Pullup hellup yiz are ninety" or "Why do I am alook alike a poss of porterpease?" or whether he managed to say exactly what he thought he was saying, but to his great astonishment, Pyla burst into tears.

"Oh, oh, oh," she wailed. "That would have been my very first coup. And you beat me, you beat me."

The jury was already in a huddle. A few moments later Silvador, the leader, stroked Pyla gently on the temples and said: "Hush now. On the contrary, our Web-friend must be penalized for lying."

His eyes twinkling, he offered Estelle his arm, and she came to her feet in one sinuous unravelling of the knot she had tied herself into during the lying game.

"The penalty must include our Estelle-friend too," he added portentously. "You must both come with us, directly to the city, and be"—he struck an executioner's pose—"put to sleep for a while."

"No," Web said. "We have to go." He clambered stiffly to his feet.

"Please," Silvador said. "We don't really mean to punish. You wanted to sleep-learn. We can take you to the sleep-learner. Is that not what you asked this morning? Pyla has two hours coming to her this afternoon. We were going to give it to you; you could learn Hevian and talk to us!"

"But how did we lie?" Estelle said, her eyes dancing.

"Web said it was good news," Silvador said solemnly, "that his Dee-friend was already here. He told a flat lie about an accomplished fact; that costs fifty points."

The two New Earth children looked at each other. "Oh, algae and gravity," Web said suddenly. "Let's go do it. We'll see Dee soon enough."

Dee blew her top.

"What on Earth were you thinking of, John?" she demanded. "How do you know what they teach in hypnopedia here? How could you let children run around a strange planet without knowing what these savages might do to them?"

"They didn't do anything to us——" Web said.

"They're not savages——" Amalfi said.

"I know what they are. I was here the first time, when you were. And I think it's criminally irresponsible to let savages tamper with a child's mind. Or any civilized mind."

"How would you recognize a civilized mind?" Amalfi demanded. But he knew that it was certainly a fruitless question, and possibly a spiteful one. He could see well enough that she was the same girl he had met during the Utopia-Gort affair, the same woman he had loved, the same bright physical image he would cherish to the nearing end of time; but she was getting old, and how do you tell a woman that? The Hevians and the children alike were approaching the end of the world as a new experience, but Dee, and Amalfi, and Mark, and indeed the whole of New Earth were approaching it from age, with no thought but to stave off new experience, to dwell safely in accomplished fact. He himself would not accept that such a thing was to happen; Dee would not let the children learn a new language; they were exhibiting all the stigmata of the onset of old age, and so was their culture. The drugs still worked; physically they were still young; but age was with them, none the less, and for good. In the long run there was no cheating time and the entropy gradient, nor any hope but that of putting one's hope into Hevians and other children. The cancer-scarred giant King of Buda-Pesht and the Acolyte jungle had been as old as Amalfi was now when Amalfi had met and bested him, and he had even then settled into an *idée fixe*; he had been still physically arrested, but mentally he was already used up.

There were only two ways to go toward death; you accept that you are going to die, or you refuse to believe it. To deny that the problem is there is childish, or senile; it lacks the fluidity of adjustment which is that process called maturity; and when children and savages are more fluid at this than you are, you must see that curfew has struck for you and go gracefully. Otherwise, they will bury you, their titular leader, nominally alive.

Dee had not, of course, bothered to answer the question; she simply looked grim. The aborted argument had been conducted mostly *sotto voce* anyhow, for the rest of the Hevian council-room was deeply embroiled in an attempt to quanticize the amount of gamma radiation which would be produced when the two universes passed through each other, and its degree of convertibility into either of the two forms of matter subsequent to the impact; Dee had been forced to push her way into the meeting to find Web and Estelle, who by now had become accepted silent partners at such skull-sessions.

"I'm not content with that at all," Retma was saying. "Dr. Schloss is assuming that a substantial part of this energy will go off as sheer noise, as though the meeting of the two universes were analogous to the clashing of cymbals. To allow that, one has to assume that Planck's Constant holds true in Hilbert space, for which we haven't a shred of evidence. One can't superimpose an entropy gradient at right angles to a reaction which itself involves entropies of opposite sign on each side of the equation."

"But why can't you?" Dr. Schloss said. "That's what Hilbert space is for: to provide a choice of axes for just such an operation. If you have such a choice, the rest is only a simple exercise in projective geometry."

"I don't deny that," Retma said, somewhat stiffly. "I'm questioning its applicability. We have no data which suggest that handling the problem in this way would be anything *more* than an exercise—so whether it would be a simple exercise or a complex exercise is not to the point."

"I think we'd better go," Dee said. "Web, Estelle, please come along; we're only interrupting, and there's a lot we have to do."

Her penetrating stage whisper rasped across the discussion more effectively than any speech at normal conversational volume could have done. Dr. Schloss's face pinched with annoyance. For a moment, the faces of the Hevians went politely blank; then Miramon turned and looked first at Dee, and then at Amalfi, slightly raising one eyebrow. Amalfi nodded, a little embarrassed.

"Do we have to go, Grandmother?" Web protested. "I mean, all this is what we're here for. And Estelle's good at math; now and then Retma and Dr. Schloss want her to match up Hevian names for terms with ours."

Dee thought about it. "Well," she said, "I suppose it can't do any harm."

This was exactly and expectably the wrong answer, though Web could have had no way of anticipating it. He did not know, as Amalfi knew very well by direct memory, that women on He had once been much worse than slaves, that in fact they had been regarded as a wholly loathesome though necessary cross between a demon and a lower animal; hence he was unequipped to see that Hevian women today were still crucially subordinate to their men, and far from welcome in a situation of this kind. Nor did Amalfi see any present opportunity to explain to Web—or to Estelle, either—why both children must now go. The explanation would require more knowledge of Dee than either of the children had; they would need to know, for instance, that in Dee's eyes the women of He had been emancipated but not enfranchised, and that for Dee this abstract distinction carried a high emotional charge—all the more so because the Hevian women themselves were obviously quite content to have it that way.

Miramon settled his papers, arose and walked smoothly toward them, his face grave. Dee watched him approach with an expression of smouldering, resolute suspicion with which Amalfi could not help but sympathize, funny though he found it.

"We are delighted to have you with us, Mrs. Hazleton," Miramon said, bowing his head. "Much of what we are today, we owe to you. I hope you will allow us to express our gratitude; my wife and her ladies await to do you honour."

"Thanks, but I don't—I didn't really mean——"

She had to stop, obviously finding it impossible to summon up in a split second the memory of what she had meant so many years ago, when she had been, whether she was yet aware of it or not, another person. Back then, she had in fact been one of the prime movers in the emancipation of the women of He, and Amalfi had been glad of her vigorous help, particularly since it had turned out to be crucial in a bloody power-struggle on the planet, and hence crucial to the survival of the city—the latter a formula which then had been as magical and beyond critical examination as the will to live itself, and now was as meaningless a slogan and one as far gone in time as "Remember the Bastille", "Mason, Dixon, Nixon and Yates", or "The Stars Must Be Ours!" Dee's first encounter with Hevian women had been in the days when they had been stinking unwashed creatures kept in ceremonial cages; something about Miramon's present mode of address to her apparently reminded her of those days, perhaps even made her feel the bars and the dirt falling into place about her own person; yet the time gap was too great, and the politeness too intensive, to permit her to take offence on those grounds, if indeed she was aware of them. She looked quickly at Amalfi, but his face remained unchanged; she knew him well enough to be able to see that there would be no help from that quarter.

"Thank you," she said helplessly. "Web, Estelle, it's time we left."

Web turned to Estelle, as if for help, in unconscious burlesque of Dee's unspoken appeal to Amalfi, but Estelle was already rising. To Amalfi's eyes the girl looked amused and a little contemptuous. Dee was going to have trouble with that one. As for Web, anyone could see plainly that he was in love, so *he* would require no special handling.

"What I suggest is this," Estelle's father's voice said, way up in the middle of the air. "Suppose we assume that there is no thermodynamic crossover between the two universes until the moment of contact. If that's the case, there's no possibility of applying symmetry unless we assume that the crossover point is actually a moment of complete neutrality, no matter how explosive it seems to somebody on one side or the other of the equivalence sign. That's a reasonable assumption, I think, and it would enable us to get rid of Planck's Constant—I agree with Retma that in a situation like this that's only a bugger factor—and handle the opposite signs in terms of the old Schiff neutrino-anti-neutrino theory of gravitation. That can be quanticized equally well, after all."

"Not in terms of the Grebe numbers," Dr. Schloss said.

"But that's exactly the point, Schloss," Jake said excitedly. "Grebe numbers don't cross over; they apply in our universe, and probably they apply on the other side too, *but they don't cross.* What we need is a function that does cross, or else some assumption that fits the facts that frees us of crossover entirely. That's what Retma was saying, if I understood him correctly, and I think he's right. If you don't have a crossover expression which is perfectly neutral anywhere in Hilbert space, then you're automatically making an assumption about a real no-man's-land. What we're forced to start with here is *No.*"

Estelle stopped at the door and turned to look toward the invisible source of the voice.

"Daddy," she said, "that's just like translating Hevian math into New Earth math. If it's no-man's-land you have to deal with, why don't you start with the bullets?"

"Come, dear," Dee said. The door closed.

There was a very long silence in the room after that.

"You are letting those children go to waste, Mayor Amalfi," Miramon said at last. "Why do you do it? If only you would fill their brains with the facts that they need—and it is so easy, as you well know, you taught us how to do it——"

"It's no longer so easy with us," Amalfi said. "We are older than you are; we no longer share your preoccupation with the essences of things. It would take too long to explain how we came to that pass. We have other things to think about now."

"If that is true," Miramon said slowly, "then indeed we must hear no more about it. Otherwise I shall be tempted to feel sorry for you; and that must not happen, otherwise we all are lost."

"Not so," Amalfi said, smiling tightly. "Nothing is ever that final. Where were we? This is only the beginning of the end."

"Were the universe to last for ever, Mayor Amalfi," Miramon said, "I should never understand you."

And so the betrayal was complete. Web and Estelle never heard the stiff and bitter exchange between Amalfi and Hazleton, across the trillions and trillions of miles of seethingly empty space between He and New Earth, which resulted in Hazleton's being forced to call his wife home before she antagonized the Hevians any further; nor did they know precisely why Dee's recall had to mean their recall. They simply went, mute and grieving, willy-nilly, expressing by silence—the only weapon that they had—their revolt against the insanities of adult logic. In their hearts they knew that they had been denied the first real thing that they ever wanted, except for each other.

And time was running out.

5

JEHAD

That conversation had been unusually painful for Amalfi, too, despite his many centuries of experience at having differences of opinion with Hazleton, ending ordinarily in enforcement of Amalfi's opinion if there was no other way around it. There had been something about this quarrel which had been tainted for Amalfi, and he knew very well what it was: the abortive, passionless and fruitless autumnal affair with Dee. Sending her home to Mark now, necessary though he believed it to be, was too open to interpretation as an act of revenge upon the once-beloved for being no longer loved. Such things happened between lovers, as Amalfi knew very well.

But there was so much to be done that he managed to forget about it after Dee and the children had left on the recall ship. He was not, however, allowed to forget about it for long—only, in fact, for three weeks.

The discussion of the forthcoming catastrophe had at last entered the stage where it was no longer possible to avoid coming to grips with the contrary entropy gradients, and hence had entered an area where words alone no longer sufficed—in fact, could seldom be called upon at all. This had had the effect of driving those participants who were primarily engineers or administrators or both, like Miramon and Amalfi, or primarily philosophers, like Gifford Bonner, into the stance of bystanders; so that the discussions now had been shifted to Retma's study. Amalfi stuck with them whenever he could, for he never knew when Retma, Jake or Schloss might drop back out of the symbolic stratosphere and say something he could comprehend and use.

It was being heavy weather in the study today, however. Retma was saying:

"The problem, as I see it is that time in our experience is not retrodictable. We write a diffusion equation like this, for instance." He turned to his blackboard—the immemorial "research instrument" of theoretical physicists everywhere—and wrote:

$$\frac{d^2G}{dx^2} + \frac{d^2G}{dy^2} + \frac{d^2G}{dz^2} = a^2 \frac{dG}{dt}$$

Over Retma's head, for Jake's benefit, a small proxy fixed its television eye on the precise chalkmarks. "In this situation a-squared is a real constant, so it is predictive only for a future time *t*, but not for an earlier time -*t*, because the retrodictive expression diverges."

"An odd situation," Schloss agreed. "It means that in any thermodynamic situation we have better information about the future than we do about the past. The footprint that Crusoe saw on the beach couldn't change his past on his island beachhead—or planetfall, if you like; but he knew it would change his future. And that's what we know about death, too. We've never known anything like it before, but we know the sands flow that way, and no other. In the anti-matter universe it has to be the other way around—but only from *our* point of view; a hypothetical observer living under their laws and composed of their energies, I assume, couldn't tell the difference."

"Can we write a convergent retrodictive equation?" Jake's voice said. "One which describes what their situation is as we would see it, if we could? If we can't, I don't see how we can design instruments to detect any difference."

"It can be done," Retma said. "For instance." He turned to the blackboard and the symbols flowed squeakily:

$$\frac{d^2G}{dx^2} + \frac{d^2G}{dy^2} + \frac{d^2G}{dz^2} = \frac{4\pi m}{ih}\frac{dG}{dt}$$

"Ah-*ha*," Schloss said. "Thus giving us an imaginary constant in place of a real one. But your second equation isn't a mirror of your first; parity is not conserved. Your first equation is an equalization process, but this one is oscillatory. Surely the gradient on the other side doesn't pulsate!"

"Parity is not conserved anyhow in these weak reactions," Jake said. "But I think the objection may be well taken all the same. If Equation Two describes anything at all, it can't be the other side. It has to be *both* sides—the whole vast system, Hell and Heaven, providing that it is cyclical, which we don't know yet. Nor do I see any way to test it, it's as ultimately and finally unprovable as the Mach Hypothesis——"

The door opened quietly and a young Hevian beckoned silently to Amalfi. He got up without too much reluctance; the boys were giving him a hard time today, and he found that he missed Estelle. It had been her function to remind the group of possible pitfalls in Retma's notation: here, for instance, Retma was using the *d* which in Amalfi's experience was an increment in calculus, as simply an expression for a constant; he was using the *G* which to Amalfi was the gravitational constant, to express a term in thermodynamics Amalfi was accustomed to seeing written with the greek capital letter ψ; and could Schloss be sure that Retma's *i* was equivalent to the square root of minus one, as it was in New Earth math? Doubtless Schloss had good reason to feel that agreement on that very simple symbol had been established between the New Earthmen and Retma long since, but without Estelle it made Amalfi feel uncomfortable. Besides, though he knew intellectually that all the important battles against a problem in physics are won in such blackboard sessions as this, he was not temperamentally fitted to them. He liked to see things happening.

They began to happen forthwith. As soon as the door was decently closed on the visible and invisible physicists, the young Hevian said:

"I am sorry to disturb you, Mr. Amalfi. But there is an urgent call for you from New Earth. It is Mayor Hazleton."

"Helleshin!" Amalfi said. The word was Vegan; no one now alive knew what it meant. "All right, let's go."

"Where is my wife?" Hazleton demanded without preamble. "And my grandson, and Jake's daughter? And where have you been these past three weeks? Why didn't you call in? I've been losing my mind, and the Hevians gave me the Force Four blowaround before they'd let me through to you at all——"

"What are you talking about, Mark?" Amalfi said. "Stop sputtering long enough to let me know what this is all about."

"That's what *I* want to know. All right. I'll begin again. Where is Dee?"

"I don't know," Amalfi said patiently. "I sent her home three weeks ago. If you can't find her, that's your problem."

"She never got here."

"She didn't? But——"

"Yes, but. That recall ship never landed. We never heard from it at all. It just vanished, Dee, children and all. I've been phoning you frantically to find out whether or not you ever sent it; now I know that you did. Well, we know what *that* means. You'd better give up dabbling in physics, Amalfi, and get back here on the double."

"What can I do?" Amalfi said. "I don't know any more about it than you do."

"You can damn well come back here and help me out of this mess."

"What mess?"

"What have you been doing the past three weeks?" Hazleton yelled. "Do you mean to tell me that you haven't heard what's been happening?"

"No," Amalfi said. "And stop yelling. What did you mean, 'We know what *that* means'? If you think you know what's happened, why aren't you doing something about it, instead of jamming the Dirac raising me? You're the mayor; I've got work of my own to do."

"I'll be the mayor about two days longer, if my luck holds," Hazleton said in a savage voice. "And you're directly responsible, so you needn't bother trying to duck. Jorn the Apostle began to move two weeks ago. He has a navy now, though where he raised it is beyond me. His main body's nowhere near New Earth, but he's about to take New Earth all the same—the whole planet is swarming with farm kids with fanatical expressions and dismounted spindillies. As soon as they get to me, I'm going to surrender out of hand—you know as well as I do what one of those machines can do, and the farmers are using them as side-arms. I'm not going to sacrifice tens of thousands of lives just to maintain my administration; if they want me out, they can have me out."

"And this is my fault? I once told you the Warriors of God were dangerous."

"And I didn't listen. All right. But they'd never have moved if it hadn't been for the fact that you and Miramon didn't censor what you're up to. It's given Jorn his cause; he's telling his followers that you're meddling with the pre-ordained Armageddon and jeopardizing their chances of salvation. He's proclaimed a jehad against the Hevians for instigating it, and the jehad includes New Earth because we're working with the Hevians——"

Over the phone came four loud, heavy strokes of fist upon metal.

"Gods of all stars, they're here already," Hazleton said. "I'll leave the line open as long as I can—maybe they won't notice. . . ." His voice faded. Amalfi hung on grimly, straining to hear every sound.

"Sinner Hazleton," a young and desperately frightened voice said, almost at once, "you have been found out. By the Word of Jorn, you—you are ordered to corrective discipline. Are you gone-tuh—will you submit humbly?"

"If you fire that thing in here," Hazleton's voice said, quite loudly—he was obviously projecting for the benefit of the mike—"you'll uproot half the city. What good will that do you?"

"We will die in the Warriors," the other voice said. It was still tense, but now that it spoke of dying it seemed more self-assured. "You will go to the flames."

"And all the other people——?"

"Sinner Hazleton, we do not threaten," a deeper, older voice said. "We think there is some good in everyone. Jorn commands us to redeem, and that we will do. We have hostages for your good conduct."

"*Where are they?*"

"They were picked up by the Warriors of God," the deep voice said. "Jorn in his blessedness was kind enough to grant us a *cordon sanitaire* for this Godless world. Will you yield, for the salvation of this woman and these two helpless children? I advise you, Sinner—hey, what the hell, that phone's open! Jody, smash that switch, and fast! What did I ever do to be saddled with a cadre of lousy yokels——"

The speaker began a thin howl and went dead before the cry was properly born.

For a moment, Amalfi sat stunned. He had gotten too much information too fast; and he was much older now than he had been on like occasions in the past. He had never expected that such an occasion would arise again—but here it was.

A jehad against He? No, not likely—at least, not directly. Jorn the Apostle would be wary of tackling a world so completely mysterious to him, especially with forces more mob than military. But New Earth was wholly vulnerable; it was a logical first step to invest that planet. And now Jorn had Dee and the children.

Move!

How to move was another matter; it needed to be done in a vessel which no possible Warrior cordon would have the strength to attack, but no such vessel existed on He. The only other alternative was a very small, very fast ship with a low detectability index; but that was equally impossible across so long a distance, since there is a minimum size for even one spindizzy. Or was there? Carrel was on He, and Carrel had had considerable experience in designing relatively small spindizzy-powered proxies; one such had followed the March on Earth all the way, without anybody's paying the slightest attention to it. Of course that proxy had been magnificently, noisily detectable by ordinary standards, and only Carrel's piloting of it had kept the massed cities from distinguishing between the traces that it made and the traces that were made adventitiously by ordinary interstellar matter. . . .

"Can you do that again, Carrel? Remember that this time you won't have a flock of massive cities to confuse the issue. The gamut you'll have to run will be one thin shell of orbiting warships, around one planet —and we don't know how many of them there are, what arms they mount, how careful a watch they keep——"

"Assume the worst," Carrel said. "They caught the recall ship, after all, and they didn't even know we'd sent it. I can do it, Mr. Amalfi, if you'll let me do the manœuvring when the chips are down; otherwise I think you'll be caught, no matter how small the ship is."

"Helleshin!" But there was no way around it; Amalfi would have to subject himself to at least two days of Carrel's violent evasive-confusive manœuvres, without once touching the spacestick himself. It was going to be a rough do for an old man, but Carrel was quite right, there was no other available course.

"All right," he said. "Just make sure I'm alive when I touch down."

Carrel grinned. "I've never lost a cargo," he said. "Providing it's been properly secured. Where do you want to land?"

That was no easy question either. In the long run, Amalfi settled for a landing in Central Park, in the heart of the old Okie city. This was perhaps dangerously close to the Warriors' centre of operations, but Amalfi did not want to be forced to trek across a thousand miles of New Earth just for a meeting with Hazleton; and there was a fair chance that the old city would be taboo for the bumpkins, or at least avoided instinctively. Jorn the Apostle would not have overlooked patrolling such an obvious rallying-point for the ousted, but presumably Jorn was somewhere at the other end of the Cloud with his main body.

Since there is, even with spindizzies, a limit to the amount of power that can be stored in a small hull, the trip was more than long enough for Amalfi to catch up, via ultraphone, on the Cloud events he had closeted himself away from on He. The picture Mark had given him had been accurate, if perhaps a little distorted in emphasis. Jorn the Apostle's real concerns were still far away from New Earth, and his jehad had been announced against unbelievers everywhere, not just against the Hevians. The Hevians were simply the article in the indictment which applied specifically to New Earth—that, and New Earth's unannounced but unconcealed intention of plumbing the end of time, which was blasphemy. It was Amalfi's guess that the uprising on New Earth and the seizure of the central government there had been an unplanned by-product of the proclamation of which Jorn was unprepared to take full advantage. Had he been planning on it, or militarily able to capitalize on it, he would have rushed in his main body on the double; as matters stood he had only—and belatedly—set up a token blockade. If his followers' coup stuck, all well and good; if it did not, he would withdraw the blockade in a hurry, to save ships and men for another, more auspicious day.

Or so Amalfi reasoned; but he was uncomfortably aware that in Jorn the Apostle he was for the first time dealing with an enemy whose thought-processes might be utterly unlike his, from first to last.

The ship shifted abruptly from spindizzy to ion-blast drive. Amalfi stopped thinking entirely and just hung on.

Once in the atmosphere, the craft was back in Amalfi's hands; back on He, Carrel had relinquished his remote Dirac control over the space-stick. Amalfi was able to make a thistledown nightside landing in south Central Park, in a broad irregular depression which legend said had once been a lake. The landing was without incident; apparently it had been undetected. In the morning the abandoned proxy might be spotted by a Warrior flyer, but the old city was littered with such ambiguous mechanical objects; one had to be a student of the city, as knowledgeable as Schliemann was about the nine Troys, to know which was new and which was not. Amalfi was confident enough of this to leave the proxy behind without any attempt to camouflage it.

Now the problem was: How to get in touch with Mark? Presumably he was still under arrest, or the next thing to it; "corrective discipline" was what the Warrior voice Amalfi had overheard had said. Did that mean that they were going to make the lazy, cerebral Hazleton make beds, sweep floors and pray six hours a day? Not very likely, especially the prayer part. Then what——

Suddenly, trudging south along a moonlit, utterly deserted Fifth Avenue toward the city's control tower, Amalfi was sure he had it. Running a galaxy, even a small and mostly unexplored satellite galaxy like this one, is not simply a matter of taking papers out of the "IN" tray and transferring them to the "OUT" tray. It requires centuries of experience and a high degree of familiarity with the communications, data-filing and other machines which must do 98 per cent of the donkey-work. In the Okie days, for instance, it sometimes happened—though not very often—that a mayor was swapped to another city under the "rule of discretion" after he had lost an election; and generally it took him five to ten years to get used to running the new one, even in such a subordinate post as assistant to the city manager. It was not an art that a bumpkin, no matter how divinely inspired, could master in a week.

Mark's most likely theatre of "corrective discipline",

then, would be his own office. He would be running the Cloud for the Warriors—and no doubt doing a far worse job of it than they would detect, even were they sensible enough, as they surely were, to suspect such sabotage. Amalfi, himself a master of making the wheels run backwards when necessary, would yield precedence in that art to Hazleton at any time; Hazleton had been known to work the trick on his friends, just to keep his hand in, or perhaps just out of habit.

Very good; then the problem of getting in touch with Mark was solved, clearing the way for the hard questions: How to discombobulate, and, if possible, oust the Warriors; and how to get Dee and the children back unharmed?

It would be difficult to decide which of these two hard questions was the harder. As Mark had pointed out, the uprooted spindillies in the hands of the rank-and-file Warriors were considerably more dangerous than muskets or pitchforks. Used with precision, the machine could degravitate a single opponent and send him shrieking skyward under the centrifugal thrust of New Earth's rotation on its axis; or the same effect could be used against a corner or a wall of a building, if one wanted to demolish a strong point. But the menace lay in the fact that in the hands of a ploughboy the spindilly would *not* be used with precision. It had been designed, not as a weapon, but as an adjunct to home weather control, and was somewhat larger, heavier and more ungainly than a twentieth-century home oil-burner. Considering the difficulties involved in toting this object at all, especially on foot, the temptation would be almost overwhelming to set it at maximum output before it was even unbolted from its cement pedestal in the cellar, and leave it set there, so that the strained arm and back muscles of the bearer would thereafter have to do nothing with it to make it function but point it—more or less—and push the starter button. This meant that every time one of the ploughboys lost his temper or detected heresy in some casual remark, or fired nervously at a shadow or a sudden unfamiliar sound or a svengali, he might level two or three city blocks before he remembered where the "kill" button was; or the machine, dropped and abandoned in panic, might go on to level two or three more blocks before it discharged its accumulators and shut itself off of its own accord.

Saving Dee and the children was certainly highly important, but disarming the Warriors would have to take precedence.

He caught himself bouncing a little as he stepped out of the spindizzy lift shaft on to the resilient concrete floor of the control room, and grinned ruefully. He felt alive again, after far too many years of grousing, browsing, vegetating. This was the kind of problem he had been formed for, the kind he approached with the confidence born of gusto. The end of time was certainly sizeable enough as a problem; he would never find a bigger, and he was grateful for that; but it provided him with nobody with whom to negotiate and, if possible, swindle a little.

It *had* been a long time; he had better be on his guard against overconfidence. That had been known to trip him now and then even when he had been in practice. In particular, it was suspiciously easy to see what steps ought to be taken in the present situation; that was not the test; it was his ancient skill as a cultural historian—in short, as a diagnostician—which would stand or fall by what he did now . . . and just incidentally, he might lose or save from three to a quarter of a million lives, one of them Estelle's.

Gently then, gently—but precisely and with decision, like a surgeon confronted with cardiac arrest. Waste no time debating alternate courses; you have four minutes to save the patient's life, if you are lucky; the bone-saw is whining in your hand—slash open the rib-cage, and slash it quick.

The City Fathers were already warmed up. He told them: "Communications. Get me Jorn the Apostle—for the survival of the city."

It would take a little while for the City Fathers to reach Jorn; though they would scan the possibilities in under a minute and select out only those worlds with high probability ratings for Jorn's presence, the chances of their getting him on the first call were not very high. Amalfi regretted that it would be then necessary to talk to Jorn on the Dirac communicator, since it would make anyone who was listening anywhere in the Cloud—or anywhere else in the known universe where the apparatus existed, for that matter—privy to the conversation; but over interstellar distances the ultraphone was out of the question for two-way exchanges, since its velocity of information propagation was only 125 per cent of the speed of light, and even this was achieved only by a trick called negative phase velocity, since the carrier wave was electromagnetic and moved at light speed and no faster.

While he waited, Amalfi ticked over the possibilities. This was all in all developing into a most curious affair, quite unlike anything he had ever been involved in before. It thus far consisted mostly of interludes and transitions, with only a small scatter of decision points upon which action might be possible. In this sense even the events which most recalled to him the events of his earlier life seemed to be reshaping themselves into the pattern of his old age, not only allowing for but requiring a much greater exercise of reflection and an intensive weighing of values. Reflexive action was out of the question; it was possible only from some fixed guiding principle, such as "the survival of the city"; such an axiom, if it persists and dominates for a long time, allows many decisions to be reached via the reflex arc with almost no intervening intellection—one automatically jumped in the right direction, like a cat turning itself over in mid-air. No such situation existed now; the values to be weighed were mutually contradictory.

It had to be assumed, first of all, that Jorn did not know the situation on New Earth in detail; he had simply reacted as a good strategist should to capitalize upon an unexpected victory in an unexpected quarter, and almost surely did not know that his blockading fleet was holding three hostages, let alone who those hostages were. It would be impossible to intimidate him on this matter; it would be wiser not to give him the information at all. After all, the first intent of the call was to get the bumpkin army disbanded and the dismounted spindillies out of action; but it would not do to convince him out of hand that his coup on New Earth could not possibly stick, since that would result in his withdrawing his blockade and the hostages with it. Better to serve both ends, if it could be swung that way: to convince Jorn that the *putsch* had better be abandoned forthwith, but not so thoroughly as to alarm him into thinking he might lose part of his navy if he took his time about calling the *putsch* off.

It looked like a large order. It meant that the danger which Jorn the Apostle would have to be made to suspect would have to be as much ideological as it was military. As a military commander of considerable proven ability, Jorn could not but be familiar with the corruption of an occupying force by the standards and customs of the nation that it occupies—and jehads and crusades were particularly subject to this kind of corrosion. Whether he was wholly a believer in the brand of Fundamentalism he preached, or not, he would not want his followers to lose faith in the doctrine under which he had sailed so successfully thus far; that was the hold over them that he had chosen to exercise, so that if they lost that, he himself would have nothing left, regardless of what his personal beliefs might be.

Unhappily, there was no ideology available on New Earth which looked capable of corrupting the Warriors of God; they would doubtless indulge in a good deal of wristwatch collecting, a very ancient term for a timeless syndrome of a peasant army holding a territory relatively rich in consumer goods, but Jorn would anticipate that and discount it; but there was no idea inherent in the culture of New Earth which seemed strong enough to sway the Warriors from their simple, direct and centrally oriented point of view. One would have to be manufactured; at least there was no lack of raw materials.

One apparent pitfall in this course was that of taking Jorn the Apostle at his own public valuation and attempting to reach into and alarm that part of his mind where his real religion lived. Amalfi had no way of knowing whether this would work or not, and prudence dictated that it not be tried; he had to assume instead that a man as successful as Jorn had been in the world of affairs was a sophisticated man on most subjects, whether he was sophisticated as a theologian or not. The latter was even beside the point; wherever the truth lay, he would be quick to detect any attempt to push his religious buttons, since he had proven that he knew the art himself.

And, Amalfi thought suddenly, if Jorn were to turn out to be exactly as devout in his back-cluster superstitions as his public utterances suggested, pushing that button might well result in a genuine disaster. With such people, that button is a demolition button; if you touch it successfully, you shatter the man. Of course it would be necessary to treat Jorn *pro forma* as if every public word Jorn had uttered had been uttered in the utmost sincerity and out of the deepest kind of belief, not only because Jorn too would know that unknown numbers of others might be listening in, but to avoid attacking the man's image of himself irrelevantly and to no purpose. The forms had no bearing on the final outcome; it would be dangerous to assume that Jorn was identical personally with his public self only in the *substance* of Amalfi's approach to him. There would be no harm in acknowledging to him, implicitly, his claim to be every inch a Fundamentalist; but it would be fatal to expect him to panic if he got a Dirac-'cast claiming to be from Satan——

"READY WITH JORN THE APOSTLE, MR. MAYOR."

Amalfi suddenly found himself thinking at emergency speed; the City Fathers' excusable lapse—doubtless nobody had bothered to tell them that Amalfi had not been Mayor since the problem of the Ginnunga-Gap had arisen—reminded him that he had failed to decide whether or not to identify himself to Jorn. There was a small possibility that Jorn came of the peasant stock which the Okies had found sweating under the tyranny of the bindlestiff city of IMT; a slightly larger possibility that he was a descendant of the rulers of IMT itself; but by far the greatest likelihood was that he was a child or grandchild of Amalfi's own people and so would know very well indeed who Amalfi was. To identify himself, then, would give Amalfi a certain leverage, but it would also present certain disadvantages——

However, the die was already cast; the City Fathers had called him the Mayor on the circuit, so Jorn had better be told at once that it was not Hazleton he was talking to. Bluff it out? Possible; but there lay the danger of using the Dirac: the instrument made it possible for any listener to tell Jorn, now or later, whatever facts Amalfi attempted for strategic reasons to withhold——

"READY, MR. MAYOR."

Well, there was no help for that now. Amalfi said into the microphone:

"Go ahead."

Immediately the screen came alight. He *was* getting old: he had forgotten to tell the City Fathers to limit the call to audio only, so in actuality he had never had the option of withholding his identity. Well, regret was futile; and in fact he watched the face of Jorn the Apostle swimming into view before him with the keenest curiosity.

It was, startlingly, a very old face, narrow, bony and

deeply lined, with bushy white eyebrows emphasizing the sunken darkness of the eyes. Jorn had been off the anti-agathics for at least fifty years, if indeed he had ever taken one. The realization was a profound and unexpected visceral shock.

"I am Jorn the Apostle," the ancient face said. "What do you want of me?"

"I think you should pull off of New Earth," Amalfi said. It was not at all what he had intended to say; it was in fact wholly contrary to the entire chain of reasoning he had just worked through. But there was something about the face that compelled him to say what was on his mind.

"I am not on New Earth," Jorn said. "But I take your meaning. And I take it there are many people on New Earth who share your opinion, Mr. Amalfi, as is only natural. This does not affect me."

"I didn't expect it to, just as a simple statement of opinion," Amalfi said. "But I can offer you good reasons."

"I will listen. But do not expect me to be reasonable."

"Why not?" Amalfi said, genuinely surprised.

"Because I am not a reasonable man," Jorn said patiently. "The uprising of my followers on New Earth took place without orders from me; it is a gift which God Himself has placed in my hand. That being the case, reason does not apply."

"I see," Amalfi said. He paused. This was going to be tougher to bring off than he had dreamed; in fact, he had his first doubt as to whether it could be brought off at all. "Are you aware, sir, that this planet is a hotbed of Stochasticism?"

Jorn's bushy eyebrows lifted slightly. "I know that the Stochastics are strongest and most numerous on New Earth," he said. "I have no way of knowing how deeply the philosophy has penetrated the populace of New Earth as a whole. It is one of the things I mean to see stamped out."

"You'll find that impossible. A mob of farm boys can't eradicate a major philosophical system."

"But how major is it?" Jorn said. "In terms of influence? I admit I have the impression that much of New Earth may be corrupted by it, but I have no certain knowledge that this is so. At the distance from New Earth that I am forced to operate, I may well be magnifying it in my mind, especially since it is so completely antithetical to the Word of God; it would be natural for me to assume that the homeland of Stochasticism is also a 'hotbed' of it. But I do not know this to be true."

"So you will risk the souls of the Warriors of God on the assumption that it is not true."

"Not necessarily," Jorn said. "Considering the forces for which you speak, Mr. Amalfi, it is so plainly to your advantage to exaggerate the influence of Stochasticism; your very use of the tool suggests that, since I cannot think you mean me any advantage. I suspect that in actuality the Stochastics, like intellectuals at all times and in all places, are largely out of touch with the general assumptions of the culture in which they are operating; and that the people of New Earth are no more Stochastics than they are Warriors of God or anything else describable as a school of thought. If any label applies, they are simply a people who are *no longer* describable as Okies."

Amalfi sat there and sweated. He had met his match and he knew it.

"And if you are wrong?" he said at last. "If Stochasticism is as ingrained on this planet as I've tried to warn you it is?"

"Then", Jorn the Apostle said, "I must take the risk. My Warriors on New Earth are farm boys, as you have pointed out. I doubt that Stochasticism will make much headway with them; they will shrug it off, as contrary to common sense. They will be mistaken in that estimate, but how could they know that? Ignorance is the defence God the Father has given them, and I think it will be sufficient."

There was the cue. Amalfi could only hope that it had not come too late.

"Very well," he said, rather more grimly than he had intended. "Events will put us both to the proof; there is no more to be said."

"No," Jorn said, "there is this much more: you may actually have meant to do me a service, Mr. Amalfi. If it so proves out, then I will give the devil his due—one must be honest even with evil, there is no other good course. What do you want of me?"

And thus the verbal sparring-match had come so quickly to full circle; and this time there was no way to remain ignorant of, let alone to evade, the purport of the question. It was not political; it was personal; and it had been intended that way from the beginning.

"You could return me three hostages which your blockading fleet is holding," Amalfi said. His mouth tasted of aloes. "A woman and two children."

"Had you asked for that in the beginning", Jorn the Apostle said, "I would have given it to you." Was it actually pity in his voice? "But you have placed their lives upon the block of your own integrity, Mr. Amalfi. So be it; if I become convinced that I must lose New Earth because of Stochasticism, I will return the three before I withdraw my blockading squadron; otherwise, not. And, Mr. Amalfi——"

"Yes?" Amalfi whispered.

"Bear in mind what is at stake, and do not let your ingenuity overwhelm you. I know well that you are fabulously inventive; but human lives should not hang upon the success of a work of art. Go with God." The screen went dark.

Amalfi mopped his forehead with a trembling hand. With his last words, Jorn the Apostle had succeeded in telling the whole story of Amalfi's life, and it had not made comfortable listening.

Nevertheless, he hesitated only a moment longer. Though Jorn had probably already seen through the improvisation which had occurred to Amalfi—late enough so that he had been unable to betray that, too, to Jorn over the Dirac for the universe to hear—there was no other course open but to try to carry it through. The alternative which Jorn had proposed actually came out to the same thing in the end: that of transforming a lie into the truth. If this was an art, as Amalfi had good reason to know it was, it was at the same time not a "work of art", but only a craft; it was Jorn himself now who was committing human lives to the dictates of a work of art, that elaborate fiction which was his religion.

Being careful, this time, to cut the screen out of the circuit in advance, Amalfi called the Mayor's office.

"This is the Commissioner of Public Safety," he told

the robot secretary. In ordinary times the machine would know well enough that there was no such office, but the confusion over there now must be such that the pertinent memory banks must by now have been bypassed; he felt reasonably confident that the phrase, a code alarm of long standing in the Okie days, would get through to Hazleton; as in fact it did in short order.

"You are late calling in," Mark's voice said guardedly. "Your report is overdue. Can't you report your findings in person?"

"The situation is too fluid to permit that, Mr. Mayor," Amalfi said. "At present I'm making rounds of the perimeter stations in the old city. Off-duty Warriors are trying to sightsee here, and of course with so much live machinery——"

"Who is that?" another voice said, farther in the background. Amalfi recognized it; it was the authoritative voice that had spotted the open phone when the Warriors had first arrested Hazleton. "We can't permit that!"

"It's the Commissioner of Public Safety, a man named de Ford," Hazleton said. Amalfi grinned tightly. De Ford had in actuality been Hazleton's predecessor as city manager; he had been shot seven centuries ago. "And of course we can't permit that. Besides all the loose energy there is about the old city, much of it is derelict. De Ford, I thought you knew that the Warriors' own general put the city off limits."

"I tell them that," Amalfi said, in a tone of injured patience. "They just laugh and say they're not Warriors on their own time."

"What!" said the heavy voice.

"That's what they say," Amalfi said doggedly. "Or

else they say that they're nobody's man but their own, and that in the long run nobody owns anybody else. They sound like they've been sitting with some Village Stochastic, though they've got it pretty garbled. I suppose the philosophers don't try to teach the pure doctrine in the provinces."

"That's beside the point," Mark said sternly. "Keep them out of the city—that's imperative."

"I'm trying, Mr. Mayor," Amalfi said. "But there's a limit to what I can do. Half of them are toting spindillies, and you know what would happen if one of those things were fired over here, even once. I'm not going to risk that."

"Be sure you don't; but keep trying. I'll see what can be done about it from this end. There'll be further instructions; where can I reach you?"

"Just leave the call in the perimeter sergeant's office," Amalfi said. "I'll pick it up on my next round."

"Very good," Hazleton said, and clicked out. Amalfi set up the necessary line from the perimeter station to the control tower and sat back, satisfied for the moment, though with a deeper uneasiness that would not go away. The seed had been planted, and there was no doubt that Hazleton had understood the move and would foster it. It was highly probable that Jorn the Apostle had already ordered an inquiry made of his officers on Earth, questioning the substance of Amalfi's claims; they would of course report back that they had had no trouble of that kind, but the inquiry itself would sensitize them to the subject.

Amalfi turned on the tower's FM receiver and tuned for New Earth's federal station. The next step would be stiffer off-limits orders to Warriors on leave, and he wanted to be sure he heard the texts. Unless Jorn's officers phrased those orders with an unlikely degree of sophistication, they would result in some actual sight-seers in the city—and of course there were no longer any perimeter sergeants, nor was there even a definable perimeter except in the minds of the City Fathers. Somebody was bound to get hurt.

That would be one incident "de Ford" would not report: "I didn't hear about it. I'm sorry, but I can't be everywhere at once. I've been trying to fend these boys off from the City Fathers—they want to ask them a lot of questions about the history of ideas that would tie the machines up for weeks. I've been telling the boys that I don't know how to operate the City Fathers, but if one of them points a spindilly at me and says 'Put me through, or else'—well——"

That speech would necessarily mark the demise of the "Commissioner of Public Safety", since it would almost surely result in the posting of a uniformed, on-duty Warrior patrol around or in the Okie city itself; Amalfi would then have to go underground, and the rest would be up to Mark. What, specifically, Hazleton would do could not be anticipated, nor did Amalfi want to know about it when it happened. One of the defects of the programme was the fact that it was, as Jorn had suspected, based on a lie, whereas a good deception ought to contain some fundamental stone of truth to stub the toes of the sane and the suspicious. To put the matter with brutal directness, there was *no* possibility that the local Warriors would be corrupted by Stochasticism, and there never had been. Even if the programme succeeded and Jorn withdrew his men, he would interrogate them closely before he gave

Amalfi back his hostages; and if everything that he found out bore Amalfi's stamp it would be too consistent to be convincing. That was why Hazleton's improvizations had to be his own from here on out, and as unknown to Amalfi as possible until it was too late for Amalfi to undo them even had he wished to.

It was indeed a poor piece of fiction upon which to hang the lives of Dee and Web and Estelle; but he had to make do with what he had.

It appeared to be working. Within the week, all Warrior leaves were cancelled in favour of special "orientation devotions" at which attendance was mandatory. Though there was no direct way to tell whether or not the Warriors resented the cancellation of their leaves to secure their faith, the predicated accident inside the city happened the next day, and the "Commissioner of Public Safety" was promptly taxed by Hazleton to explain how he had allowed it to happen; Amalfi trotted forth the prepared lie, and retreated to an ancient communications sub-station deep in the bowels of the City Fathers themselves.

The Warrior patrol was roving through the Okie city the very next day, and Amalfi was isolated; the rest had to be up to Hazleton.

By the end of that week, the Warriors had been ordered to turn in their spindillies for regulation police stun-guns, and Amalfi knew that he had won. When a conquering army is disarmed by its own officers, it is through; in a while it will begin to tear itself apart, with very little help from outside. When that order of the day got back to Jorn, he would act, and act rapidly; Hazleton had evidently been a little too thorough, as was his custom. But there was nothing that Amalfi could do now but wait.

The last Warrior blockade ship had barely touched down before Web and Estelle were scrambling out of the airlock and making straight for Amalfi.

"We have a message for you," Estelle said, out of breath, her eyes preternaturally wide. "From Jorn the Apostle. The ship's captain said to bring it to you right away."

"All right, there's not that much hurry," Amalfi growled, to hide his apprehension. "Are you all right? Did they take proper care of you?"

"They didn't hurt us," Web said. "They were so proper and polite, I wanted to kick them. They kept us in a stateroom and gave us tracts to read. It got pretty boring after a while, just reading tracts and playing tic-tac-toe on them with grandmother." Suddenly, he could not help grinning at Estelle; obviously he had gotten away with something in those quarters, all the same.

Amalfi felt a vague emotional twinge, though he was unable to identify just what kind of emotion it was; it passed too quickly. "All right, good," he said to Estelle. "Where's the message?"

"Here." She passed over a yellow flimsy, torn from the ship's Dirac printer. It said:

XXX CMNDR SSG GABRIEL SPG

32 JOHN AMALFI N EARTH V HSTGS RPT 32

I AM GIVING YOU BENEFIT OF DOUBT. RPT DOUBT. YOU ALONE KNOW TRUTH. IF THIS DEFEAT SOLELY YOUR INVENTION BE SURE THE END IS NOT YET. BUT IT WILL BE SOON.

JORN APOSTLE OF GOD

Amalfi crumpled the flimsy and dropped it on to the flaked concrete of the spaceport.

"And so it will," he said.

Estelle looked down at the wad of yellow paper, and then back at Amalfi's sombre face. "Do you know what he means?" she said.

"Yes, I know what he means, Estelle. But I hope you never do."

6

OBJECT 4001-ALEPHNULL

Nor did Estelle ever know—though in the long run she was in no doubt about it in her own mind—that the first break in thc problem of how to cross the information-barrier of the coming Ginnunga-Gap sprang from her suggestion to her father that to know no-man's-land, one must study it with bullets. Web and Estelle were, after all, only children, and in the ensuing years nobody had any time to spare for children; they were too far gone in the fever of putting together the immaterial object which would be their bullet across no-man's-land into the vast, complementary, opposite infinity of the universe of anti-matter. For the time being, speculation had been abandoned in favour of fact-finding; what was needed was some direct assessment of the contemporary energy level of the anti-matter universe; once that was known, one could hope to date precisely the coming moment of catastrophe, and know how much or how little time one had left to make such preparations for going down into death as one could bring oneself to think meaningful in the face of an imminent and complete cancellation of all meaning—and of the time of experience which alone gave meaning to the concept of meaning.

Object 4001-Alephnull

Nobody had any time for children; and so they grew up ignored, the last children that the universe would ever see. It was not surprising that they clung to each other; they would have done so even under other circumstances, for there was no question but that the fates which brood in the sub-microscopic coils and toils of the nucleic acids of heredity had formed them for each other.

Estelle sprouted in her world of oblivious adults, and took her place among them, without their noticing what she had become: tall, willowy, grey-eyed, black-haired, white-skinned, serene-faced and beautiful. These oldsters were as immune to beauty as they were immune to youth; they were perfectly happy to have the use of the sharp cutting edge of Estelle's gift for mathematics brought to bear upon their problems, but they did not see that she was also beautiful and would not have cared had they been able to see it. These days they saw nothing but death—or thought they saw it; Estelle was not so sure that they saw it as clearly as she did, for they had lived in contempt of it far too long.

Web did not know whether this suited him or not. He was moderately content to be the only one on New Earth with the good sense to see that Estelle was beautiful, but sometimes his pride felt the lack of an occasional glance of frank envy; and sometimes he suspected that Estelle cared as little about this in the long run as everyone else on New Earth but Web himself. In the fullness of time, the love which existed between them had been spoken and acknowledged, and they were now a couple, with all the delights and the responsibilities which coupling provides and demands; but somehow, nobody had noticed. The oldsters were too busy building their artifact to notice, let alone care much one way or the other, that a small green weed of love had pushed itself up amid the tumbled stones of the last of all débâcles.

Yet it was not difficult for Web to understand why what was for him a miracle was not even a nuisance to the busy godlings and their machines with whom he had to live. There was not much time left; hardly a hiccup for Amalfi and Miramon and Schloss and Dee and even for Carrel, who seemed to be a perpetually young man yet who had lived lifetimes and lifetimes and could be cut down in the midst of his latest without any valid claim that his death would be a grievous waste of whatever (and Web was convinced that it was rather scanty) he carried in his head. What little time remained would be nothing to those people, who had lived so long already; but for Web and Estelle, it had been and would continue to be their growing-up time, which would be half of each of their lives no matter how long they lived thereafter.

Certainly Amalfi never noticed them. He had long forgotten that he had ever been anything less than what he was: an immortal. Probably—now—the suggestion that he had once been a child would have baffled him entirely; in the abstract it was a truism, and he would be unable to think back far enough to think of it otherwise. Once given the administration of Doom, in any event, he prosecuted it single-mindedly, like any other job, leading toward any other destination; if he knew that there would be no other jobs and no other destinations after these, it did not seem to bother him. He was up and doing; that was enough.

In the meantime:

"I love you," Web said.

"I love you."

Around them the potsherds did not even give back an echo.

Amalfi had an excuse, had someone suggested to him that he needed one: the building of the missile had gone badly from the moment—triggered by Estelle, though he did not remember this—they had decided to give it priority. At that outset it had looked so much simpler than trying to settle all the theoretical questions *a priori*, and it had had the immediate appeal of action; but it is impossible to design an experiment without certain fundamental assumptions as to what the experiment is intended to test; which assumptions turned out to be largely absent in the supposedly practical matter of designing the anti-matter missile.

As it eventually worked out, the inter-universal messenger had to be constructed from the sub-microscopic level on up out of fundamental nuclear particles which came as close to being nothing at all as either universe would ever be likely to provide: zero-spin particles with various charges and masses, and neutrino/anti-neutrino pairs. Even detecting that the object was present at all after it had been built was an almost impossible task, for neutrinos and anti-neutrinos have no mass and no charge, consisting instead partly of spin, partly of energy of translation; it did no good to try to visualize such particles, since like all the fundamental particles they were entirely outside of experience in the macroscopic world. Matter was so completely transparent to them that stopping an average neutrino in flight would require a lead barrier fifty light-years thick.

Object 4001-Alephnull

Only the fact that the spindizzies exercised a firm control over the rotation and the magnetic moment of any given atomic particle—hence their nickname—made it possible to assemble the object at all, and to detect and direct it after it was finished. As assembled, the messenger was a stable, electrically neutral, massless plasmoid, a sort of gravitational equivalent of ball lightning; it was derived theoretically, as Jake had proposed, from the Schiff theory of gravitation, which had been advanced as long ago as 1958 but had later been abandoned for its failure to satisfy three of the six fundamental tests which the then-established theory—general relativity—seemed to satisfy very well.

"Which from our point of view is a positive advantage," Jake had argued. "The objections from general relativity are one with the dodo anyhow, and in our special case an object which would be Lorenz-invariant, as a Schiff object couldn't be, would be a drawback. Another thing: one of the tests the Schiff theory did pass was that of explaining the red shift in the spectra of distant galaxies; which we now know to have been a clock effect and not a fair test of a gravitational theory at all. We'd be better off re-evaluating the whole scholium in the light of our present knowledge."

The result was now before them all in the midst of the Okie city's ancient reception room in City Hall, which had once been Amalfi's communications centre for complex diplomatic relations with client planets; it had been fitted out with an electronic network of considerable complexity so that multiple negotiations could be carried on at once while the city approached a highly developed, highly civilized star system; now that net had become, instead, a telemetering system for the inter-universal messenger.

Since the object itself was in effect little more than an intricately structured spherical spindizzy screen which screened nothing material, it would have been impossible to see it at all were it not for the small jet of artificial smoke which issued from the floor directly under it and was wreathed about it by convection currents, making it look a little like a huge bubble being supported in the middle of a fountain. Scattered throughout the interior of the bubble were steady hot pinpoints of coloured light: concentrations of electron gas, of stripped nuclei, of thermal neutrons, of free radicals and of as many other basic test situations as the combined brains of two very different worlds had been able to contrive and to fit into so restricted a space—for the sphere was only six feet in diameter. At the very heart, in a spindizzy eddy all its own, was the greatest triumph of all: one cubical crystal of anti-sodium anti-chloride about the size of a single grain of a fine-grain photograph. This was Dr. Schloss's long-dreamt-of anti-matter artifact; here, it was a miracle which was already minus two weeks "young" and had yet a week to go in its spindizzy vacuum before it would collide with the flying instant of the present and decay; on the other side, it would be only a single crystal of common table salt, which might or might not lose its savour on the return journey—should the messenger come back to them at all.

Amalfi watched the red hand of the clock—the only hand it had—tick its quarter-seconds toward Zero. Nobody would launch the missile—exact timing was far too critical to allow that—but he had been given the privilege of holding down the key which kept the circuit closed against the moment when the red hand touched Zero and the impulse surged through the spindizzies and impelled the messenger on its way out of space, out of time, out of the humanly comprehensible entirely. No one knew what would happen then, least of all the designers. The missile would be unable to report back; once it had crossed the barrier, it would be incommunicado. It would have to come back to this great dark room before the tiny shining stars and the microscopic salt crystal inside it could report what had happened to them during the outward swing. How long that would take would depend upon the energy level on the opposite side, which was one of the things the messenger was being sent to find out; hence no transit-time could be predicted.

"We ought to give it a name," Amalfi said, fidgeting slightly. The index and middle fingers of his right hand were beginning to ache; he realized that he had been pushing down on the key for a long time with far more pressure than was necessary, as though the universe would end at once were the straining of his hand and arm to falter for an instant. Nevertheless, he did not let up; he had the good sense to realize that fatigue had already made him unable to judge how much relaxation might result, and he was not going to risk breaking the contact. "Now that we have it built, it doesn't look like anything. Let's christen it quick, before it gets away from us; it may never come back."

"I'd be afraid to give it a name," Gifford Bonner said, with a ghastly smile. "Any name we could give it would promise too much. How about a number? Back at the beginning of spaceflight, when the first unmanned satellites were going up, they numbered them like comets or other celestial objects, with the year-date and a Greek letter; the first sputnik, for instance, was called Object 1957-*a*."

"That appeals to me," Jake said. "Except for the Greek letter. This thing ought not to be indexed with any character that's ever been used before to label a known or knowable situation. How about using the trans-finite integers?"

"Very good," Gifford Bonner said. "Who will do the honours?"

"I will," Estelle said. She stepped forward. She did not dare to touch the object, but she raised her hand toward it. "I christen thee *Object 4001-Alephnull*."

"The next one, presuming that we're so lucky," Jake said, "can be Object 4001-C, which is the power of the *continuum*; and the next one——"

There was a soft chime. Startled, Amalfi looked up at the clock. The red hand was just passing over the third quartile of the first second after Zero. In the centre of the room, the smoke spun in a turbulent spiral; the bubble with the pinpoint lights had vanished.

Object *4001-Alephnull* had departed without anyone's seeing it go.

Some quartiles of a second later, he remembered to let go of the key. His millennium-firmed right hand continued to tremble for the next fifteen minutes.

The suspense was dreadful. Certainly nobody expected the messenger to return within a few hours, or even within a few days; were that to happen, it would mean that the Ginnunga-Gap itself would be right on its heels, leaving no time to analyse the coloured stars or indeed do anything but fold one's hands and wait to be snuffed out. Yet the mere fact that that very possibility existed was enough to guarantee the maintenance of a death-watch in the huge, dark old room—a death-watch enlivened by the discovery that all the instruments which had been watching the missile while it was still there had dropped back to nothing on the instant of its departure, having recorded no phenomenon of any kind about the departure itself. Not even the spindizzies—as interpreted for by the City Fathers—were prepared to say how the surge of power with which they had launched the messenger had been applied; which should have been reassuring, at least as negative evidence that the messenger had not been shoved off in some known and hence useless direction, but which under the circumstances only added to the gloom and tension. All that power shot; and where had it gone? Apparently nowhere at all.

Ordinarily Amalfi rarely dreamed (or rather, like most Okies, he dreamed most of every night, but remembered what he had dreamt in the morning less often than once every few years); but these nights were haunted by that spherical smoke-wreathed ghost with the glowing Argus eyes, wandering in a maze of twisted ingeodesics from which it would never escape, in its centre a tiny crystalline figurine piping in Amalfi's voice,

I grow not out of salt nor out of soil
But out of that which pains me

until the ingeodesics suddenly snapped into a strangling web which burned like fire, and in an explosion of light Amalfi saw that it was—no, not morning yet, but time to go back to the death-watch.

But he was already there; he had dozed off, and had been awakened by the clamour of the alarms. Now that he was more or less awake, the noise was ominously less loud then he knew it should be; there was an alarm for every star inside the messenger, and less than a third of them were ringing. The ghostly sphere floated again in the centre of the room, now no bigger than a basketball, most of its Argus-eyes out, and those that remained glowing as fitfully as corpse-fires. For all Amalfi knew, this ghost of a ghost, with so many ashes cold and cruel on its internal hearths, was no more ominous than any other outcome of a scientific experiment; it might even be promising; but he could not rid himself this early of the dread which had informed the dream.

"That was fast," Jake's voice said.

"Pretty fast," Dr. Schloss's voice said. "But now that it's back home, it's got only about twenty-one hours of life left. Let's get those readings—there's not much time."

"I'm counting down the probes now. The cameras are rolling."

Inside the ghost, another star died. There was a brief silence; then one of Dr. Schloss's technicians said, in a neutral voice: "Pi-meson shower from the iron nucleus. Looks like a natural death. No—not quite: high on the gamma side."

"Mark. The rhodium-palladium series should go next. Watch out for diagonal disintegration; it may cross with the iron series——" A star flared and burst.

"There it goes!"

"Mark," Schloss said, squinting through a gamma-ray polariscope.

"Got it. Cripes. It crossed at cesium; what does that mean?"

"Never mind, mark it. Don't stop to interpret, just record."

The ghost seemed to shiver and shrink a little. A pure, piercing tone came from its heart, wavered, and died; but it died scooping upward toward the inaudible.

"First hour," Schloss said. "Twenty to go. How long did the pip take?"

There was no answer for several minutes; then another voice said: "We don't have it down to jiffies yet. But it was short by nearly forty micro-seconds, and it Dopplered the wrong way. It's decaying in time, Dr. Schloss—it may not last as long as ten hours."

"Give me the decay rate in jiffies on the next pip and don't miss it. If it's going that fast we'll have to recalculate all the emission records on the decay curve. Jake, are you getting anything on the RF band?"

"Masses of stuff," Jake said, preoccupied. "Can't make anything of it yet. And it's scooping—that's your decay-rate again, I suspect. What a scramble!"

In this wise the second hour flew by, and then the third. Shortly thereafter, Amalfi lost track of them. The tension, the disorder, the accumulating fatigue, the utter strangeness of the experiment itself and its object, the forebodings all took their toll. These were certainly the worst possible conditions under which to gather even routine data, let alone take readings on an experiment of this degree of criticality, but once again the Okies had to make do with what they had.

"All right, everyone," Schloss said at last. "Closing time." His brow was deeply furrowed; that frown had been growing line by line during most of the final twelve hours. "Stand well back; the artifact will be the last to go."

The investigators and spectators alike—or those few spectators whose interest had been intent enough to keep them there throughout the entire proceedings—drew back to the walls of the gloomy chamber. The spindizzy whine beneath them rose slightly in both pitch and volume, and the ghost that was *Object 4001-Alephnull* disappeared behind a spindizzy screen polarized to complete opacity.

At first the spherical screen was mirror-like, throwing back grotesquely distorted images of the silent onlookers. Then a pinprick of light appeared in its centre, growing soundlessly to a painful blue-white intensity. It threw out long cobwebs and runners of glare, probing, anastomosing, flowing along the inner surface of the screen. Automatically, Amalfi shielded his eyes and his genitals in an instinctive gesture of all mankind more than two millennia old. When he was able to look again, the light had died.

The spindizzies stopped and the screen went down. Air rushed into it. *Object 4001-Alephnull* was gone, this time for ever, destroyed by the death of a single crystal of salt.

"Our precautions were insufficient; my fault," Schloss said, his voice harsh. "We are all well over our maximum permissible dose of hard radiation; everyone report to the hospital on the double for treatment. Troops, fall in!"

The radiation sickness was mild; bone-marrow transfusions brought the blood-forming system back into normal function before serious damage was done, and the nausea was reasonably well controlled by massive doses of meclizine, riboflavin and pyridoxine. All the participants who had any hair to lose lost it, including both Dee and Estelle, but they all got it back in due course except for Amalfi and Jake.

The second degree sunburn was not mild. It held up the interpretation of the results for nearly a month, while the scientists, coated in anaesthetic ointment, sat about on the wards in hospital robes and played bad poker and worse bridge. In between post-mortems on the bridge hands, they speculated endlessly and covered square miles of paper with equations and ointment grease-spots. Web, who had not lasted long enough to be present at the destruction of the crystal of salt, visited daily with bouquets for Estelle—the star-gods alone knew where and how he had unearthed so antique a custom—and fresh packs of cards for the men. He took away the spotted sheets of equations and fed them to the City Fathers, who invariably said: "NO COMMENT. THE DATA ARE INSUFFICIENT." Everyone knew that already.

At long last, however, Schloss and Jake and their crews were freed from their sticky pyjamas to tackle the mountains of raw information awaiting them. They worked long hours; Schloss in particular never remembered to eat, and had constantly to be reminded by his technicians that they had missed lunch and it was now past dinner-time. In Schloss's defence, however, it had to be admitted that this crew was the hungriest in the history of physics, and the lunch they had missed usually was just the formal meal they were accustomed to consuming after they had emptied the fat packages they brought into the laboratories; in proof of which, they all gained five or ten pounds while they were complaining the loudest.

A month after their discharge from the hospital, Schloss, Jake and Retma called a joint conference. Schloss had back the frown he had worn during the last twelve hours of the experiment, and even the traditionally impassive Hevian looked disturbed. Amalfi's heart turned over in his chest at his first glimpse of their expressions; they seemed to confirm every foggy apprehension of his dream.

"We have two pieces of bad news, and one piece of news which is wholly ambiguous," Schloss said, without any preliminaries. "I don't myself know in exactly what order I ought to present them; in that, I'm being guided by Retma and Dr. Bonner. It is their judgment that you all ought first to know that we have competition."

"Meaning what?" Amalfi said. The mere idea, empty of detail, made him prick up his ears; perhaps that was why Retma and Bonner had wanted it placed first.

"Our missile recorded clear evidence of another body in the same complicated physical state," Schloss said. "No such object could conceivably be natural in either universe; and this one was enough like ours to make us sure it came originally from our side."

"Another missile?"

"Without any doubt—and about twice the size of ours. Somebody else in our universe has found out what the Hevians found out, and is investigating the problem further along the same lines that we are—except that they appear to have had a head start of three to five years."

Amalfi pursed his lips soundlessly. "Any way of guessing who they are?"

"No. We guess that they must be relatively near by, either in our own main galaxy or in Andromeda or one of its satellites. But we can't document that; it's below the five per cent level of probability, according to the City Fathers. All the other alternatives are *way* below five per cent, but where no solution is statistically significant, we aren't entitled to choose between them."

"The Web of Hercules," Amalfi said. "It can't be anything else."

Schloss spread his hands helplessly. "It could well be anybody else, for all we know," he said. "My intuition says just what yours says, John; but there's no reliable evidence."

"All right. That's the ambiguous news, I gather. What's the first piece of bad news?"

"You've already had it," Schloss said. "It's the second piece of news, which is ambiguous, that makes the first piece bad. We've argued a long time about this, but we're now in at least tentative agreement. We think that it is possible—barely possible—to survive the catastrophe."

Quickly, Schloss held up one hand, before the stunned faces before him could even begin to lighten with hope. "Please," he said. "Don't overestimate what I say in the least. It's only a possibility, a very dim one, and the kind of survival involved will be nothing like human life as we know it. After we've described it to you, you may all much prefer to die instead. I will tell you flatly that that would be my preference; so this is not a white hope by any means. It looks black as the ace of spades to me. But—it exists. And it is what makes the news about the competition bad news. If we decide to adopt this very ambiguous form of survival, we must go to work on it immediately. It's possible only under a single very fleeting set of conditions which will hold true only for micro-seconds, in the very bowels of the catastrophe. If our unknown competitors get there first —and bear in mind that they have a good head start— they will capture it instead, and close us out. It will be a real race, and a killing one; and you may not think it worth the pace."

"Can't you be more specific?" Estelle said.

"Yes, Estelle, I can. But it will take quite a few hours to describe. Right now, what you need to know is this: If we choose this way out, we will lose our homes, our worlds, our very bodies; we will lose our children, our friends, our wives, and every vestige of companionship we have ever known; we will each of us be alone, with a thoroughness beyond the experience or the imagination of any human being in the past. And quite possibly this ultimate isolation will kill us anyhow—or if it does not, we will find ourselves wishing desperately that it had. We should all make very sure that we want to survive that badly—badly enough to be thrown into hell for eternity—not Jorn the Apostle's hell, but a worse one. It's not a thing we should decide here and now."

"Helleshin!" Amalfi said. "Retma, do you concur? Is it going to be as bad as that?"

Retma turned upon Amalfi eyes which were silver and unblinking.

"Worse," he said.

The room was very quiet for a while. At last, Hazleton said:

"Which leaves us one piece of bad news left. That must be a dilly, Dr. Schloss; maybe we'd better have it right away."

"Very well. That is the date of the catastrophe. We got excellent readings on the energy level on the other side, and we are all agreed on the interpretation. The date will be on or around June second, year Four Thousand and Four."

"The end?" Dee whispered. "Only three years away?"

"Yes. That will be the end. After that June second, there will be no June third, for ever and ever."

"And so," Hazleton said to the people in his living-room, "it seemed to me that we ought to have a farewell dinner. Most of you are leaving, with He, tomorrow morning, for the metagalactic centre. And those of you that are leaving are mostly my friends of hundreds of years, that I'll never see again; for me, when June second comes, time will have a stop—whatever apotheosis you may go on to. That's why I asked you all to eat and drink with me tonight."

"I wish you'd change your mind," Amalfi said, his voice heavy with sorrow.

"I wish I could. But I can't."

"I think you're making a mistake, Mark," Jake said solemnly. "Nothing important remains to be done on New Earth now. The future, what little's left of it, is on He. Why stay behind and wait to be snuffed out?"

"Because," Hazleton said, "I'm the mayor here. I know that doesn't seem important to you, Jake. But it's important to me. One thing that I've discovered in the last few months is that I'm not cut out to take the apocalyptic view of ordinary events. What counts with me is that I run normal human affairs pretty well—nothing more. That's what I was made for. Besting Jorn the Apostle was something that gave me great pleasure, and no matter that Amalfi set it up for me, it was fun, the kind of operation that makes me feel alive and operating at the top of my form. I'm not interested in trying to avert the triumph of time. That's not my kind of adversary. I leave that to the rest of you; I'd better stay here."

"Do you *like* to think", Gifford Bonner said, "that no matter how well you administer the Cloud, it will all be snuffed out on June second three years from now?"

"No; not exactly," Mark said. "But I shan't mind having the Cloud in the best shape I can manage when that time comes. What can I contribute to the triumph of time, Gif? Nothing. All I can do is put my world in order for that moment. That's the thing that I do—and that's why I don't belong aboard He."

"You didn't use to be so modest," Amalfi said. "You would have bailed the universe out with the Big Dipper, once, on the first excuse."

"Yes, I would," Hazleton said. "But I'm older and saner now; and so, good-bye to that nonsense. Go stop the triumph of time, John, if you can—but I know I can't. I'll stay where I am and stop Jorn the Apostle, which is as tough a problem as I care to tackle these days. The gods of all stars be with you all—but I stay here."

"So be it," Amalfi said. "At least I know at last what the real difference is between us. Let's drink to it,

Mark, and *ave atque vale*—tomorrow we turn down an empty glass."

They all drank solemnly, and there was a brief silence.

At last Dee said: "I'm staying too."

Amalfi turned and looked directly at her for the first time since they had last been together on He; they had been rather pointedly avoiding each other since their painful joint fiasco.

"That hadn't occurred to me," he said. "But of course it makes sense."

"You're not required, Dee," Mark said. "As I've said before."

"If I were, I wouldn't stay," Dee said, smiling slightly. "But I've learned a few things on He—and on board the Warrior blockader, too. I feel a little out of date, just like New Earth; I think I belong here. And that's not the only reason."

"Thanks," Mark said huskily.

"But", Web Hazleton said, "where does that leave us?"

Jake laughed. "That ought to be clear enough," he said. "Since you and Estelle made the big decision by yourselves, you don't need us to tell you how to make little ones. I'd like to have Estelle stay home with me——"

"Jake, you're not going either?" Amalfi said in astonishment.

"No. I told you before, I hate this careering about the universe. I don't see any reason why I ought to go rushing madly to the metagalactic centre to meet a doom that will find me just as handily in my own living-room. Schloss and Retma will tell you that they don't need me any more, either; I've given my best to this project, and that's an end to it; I think I'll see how far I can get on cross-breeding roses in this villainous climate before the three years are up. As for my daughter, as I was trying to say, I'd like to have her here with me, but she's already left home in the crucial sense—and this last Hevian flight is as natural to her as it's unnatural to Dee and me. In your own words, Amalfi, so be it."

"Good. We can use you, Estelle, that's for sure. Want to come?" Amalfi said.

"Yes," she said softly, "I do."

"I hadn't thought of this," Dee said in an uncertain voice. "Of course it means Web will go too. Do you think that's wise? I mean——"

"My parents don't object," Web said. "And I notice they weren't invited here tonight, grandmother."

"We didn't shut them out on your account, if that's what you're thinking," Mark said quickly. "Your father's our son, after all, Web. We were trying to confine the party to those of us who were in on the project—otherwise it would have been unmanageably large."

"Maybe so," Web said. "That's how it looks to you, I'm sure, grandfather. But I'll bet grandmother didn't think of her objections to my going on He just now."

"Web," Dee said, "I won't hear any more of that."

"All right. Then I'm going with He."

"I didn't say that."

"You don't have to say it. The decision is mine."

Most of the rest of the party had invented reasons for side conversation by this time; but both Amalfi and Hazleton were staring at Dee, Amalfi with suspicion, Hazleton with bafflement and a little hurt. "I don't understand your objection, Dee," Hazleton said. "Web's his own man now. Naturally he'll go where he thinks best—especially if Estelle's going there."

"I don't think he ought to go," Dee said. "I don't care whether you understand my reasons or not. I suppose Ron did give him permission—whether he's our son or a stranger, Mark, you know damn well that Ron's always been short on firmness—but I'm absolutely opposed to committing children to a venture like this."

"What difference can it make?" Amalfi said. "The end will come all the same, on He and on New Earth, and at the selfsame moment. With us, Web and Estelle might have a fractional chance of survival; do you want to deny them that?"

"I don't believe in this chance of survival," Dee said.

"Neither do I," Jake cut in. "But I won't deny it to my daughter on that account. I don't believe her soul will be damned unless she becomes a convert of Jorn, either—but if she wants to become a convert of Jorn, I won't forbid it to her because I think it's nonsense. What the hell, Dee, I might be wrong."

"Nobody", Web said between white lips, "can forbid me anything now on the grounds that I'm somebody's relative. Mr. Amalfi, you're the boss on this project. Am I welcome on board He, or not?"

"You are as far as I'm concerned. I think Miramon will concur."

Dee glared at Amalfi; but as he stared steadily back, she turned her glance away.

"Dee," Amalfi said, "let's call an intermission. I could be wrong about these kids too. I have a better suggestion than this squabbling: let's put it up to the

City Fathers. It's a very pleasant night outside, and I think we'd all like a walk through our old city before we say good-bye to each other and go to face armageddon in our various ways. I'd like Dee to come with me, since I won't see her again; the kids would probably like to do without our picking their bones for an hour or so; and maybe Mark would like to talk to Ron and his wife—but you can all sort yourselves out to your own tastes, I don't mean to make matches. What does everyone think of the idea?"

Oddly, it was Jake who spoke first. "I hate that damned town," he said. "I was a prisoner on board it far too long. But by God I would like to take one more look at it. I used to walk through it trying to find some place to kick it where it would hurt; I never did. Since then I've been sneering at it because it's dead and I'm alive—but the day of levelment is coming. Maybe I ought to make my peace with it."

"I feel a little like that myself," Hazleton admitted. "I had no plans to go over there before the end—and yet I don't want to let the old hulk go by default. Maybe now is the best time; after all, I was the one who called these celebrants together to begin with; let's be ceremonial, then, before we're all too busy to think about it any more."

"Web? Estelle? Will you go by what the City Fathers say?"

Web looked into Amalfi's face, and apparently was reassured at least partially by what he saw there. "On one condition," he said. "Estelle goes where she wants to go, whatever the City Fathers say. If they say there's no room for me aboard He, all right; but they can't say that to Estelle."

Estelle opened her mouth, but Web lifted his palm before her face and she subsided, kissing the base of his thumb instead. Her face was pale but serene; Amalfi had never before seen such a pure distillation of bloodless, passionate confidence as lay over her exquisite features. It was a good thing she was Web's, for again, for the fiftieth time, Amalfi's slogging brutal tireless heart was swollen with sterile love.

"Very good," he said. He offered Dee his arm. "Mark, with your permission?"

"Of course," Hazleton said; but when Dee took Amalfi's arm, his eyes turned as hard as agate. "We'll meet at the City Fathers' at 0100."

"I didn't expect this of you, John," Dee said, under the moonlight in Duffy Square. "Isn't it a little late?"

"Very late," Amalfi agreed. "And 0100 isn't far away. Why are you staying with Mark?"

"Call it belated common sense." She sat down against an ancient railing and looked up at the blurred stars. "No, don't, that's not what it is. I love him, John, for all his neglects and his emptinesses. I'd forgotten that for a while, but it's so. I'm sorry, but it's so."

"I wish you were a little sorrier."

"Oh? Why?"

"So you'd believe what you're saying," Amalfi said harshly. "Face it, Dee. It was a great romantic decision until you realized that Web would be going with me. You're still looking for surrogates. You didn't make it with me. You won't make it with Web, either."

"What a bastardly thing to say. Let's go; I've heard enough."

"Deny it, then."

"I deny it, damn you."

"You'll withdraw your objections to Web's going with me on He?"

"That has nothing to do with it. It's a filthy accusation and I won't listen to another word about it."

Amalfi was silent. The moonlight streamed down on Father Duffy's face, toneless and enigmatic. Nobody, not even the City Fathers, knew who Father Duffy had been. There was an old splash of blood on his left foot, but nobody knew how that had gotten there, either; it had been left there just in case it was historic.

"Let's go."

"No. It's early yet; they won't be there for another hour. Why do you want Web to stay on New Earth? If I'm wrong, then tell me what's right."

"It's none of your damned business, and I'm tired of this whole subject."

"It's wholly my business. I need Estelle. If Web stays here, she stays here."

"You", Dee said in a voice of bitter, dawning triumph, "are in love with Estelle! Why, you self-righteous——"

"Mind your tongue. I am in love with Estelle—and I'll lay no more finger on her than I ever laid on you. I've loved many more women than you ever managed to manœuvre into your voyeur's household, most of them before you were even born; I know the difference between love and possession—I learned it the hard way, whereas I can't see that you ever learned it at all. You are going to learn it tonight, that I promise you."

"Are *you* threatening *me*, John?"

"You're damned well right I am."

At Tudor Tower Place, bridging 42nd Street at First Avenue, looking toward the bare plaza where the UN Building had fallen in a shower of blood and glass a thousand years ago:

"I love you."

"I love you."

"I will go wherever you go."

"I will go wherever you go."

"No matter what the City Fathers say?"

"No matter what the City Fathers say."

"Then that's all we need."

"Yes. That's all we need."

In the control tower:

"They're late," Hazleton said, a little fretfully. "Oh, well, it's an easy town to get lost in."

Duffy Square:

"You wouldn't like it if I changed my mind and came with you."

"I don't want you. I'm interested only in the kids."

"You can't call my bluff, John; I don't bluff. As of now, I'm going along."

"And so are the kids?"

"No."

"Why not?"

"Because I think they'd be better off not on the same planet with—either of us."

"That's a fair start. But it's only a start. I don't care whether you go or stay, but I will have Web and Estelle."

"I thought you would. But you can't have them without me."

"And Mark?"

"If he wants to go."

"He doesn't, and you know it."

"How can you be so sure? You could be just wishing."

Amalfi laughed. Dee balled her left fist and hit him furiously on the bridge of the nose.

Tudor Tower Place:

"It's time to go."

"No. No."

"Yes, it is."

"Not yet. Not quite yet."

". . . All right. Not quite yet."

"Are you sure? Are you really sure?"

"Yes I am, oh yes I am."

"No matter what the . . ."

"No matter what they say. I'm sure."

The control tower:

"There you are," Hazleton said. "What happened, did you have an accident? You look mussed to the eyebrows."

"You must have run into a doorknob, John," Jake added. He stuttered out his parrot's chuckle. "Well, you came to the right town for it. I don't know where else in the universe you could find a doorknob."

"Where are the children?" Dee said, in a voice as dangerously even as the surface of 12-gauge armour plate.

"Not here yet," Hazleton said. "Give them time—they're afraid the City Fathers may separate them, so naturally they're staying together until the last minute. What did you fall into, anyhow, Dee? Was it serious?"

"No." Her face shut down. Bewildered, Hazleton looked from her to Amalfi and back again. It seemed as though the mouse over Amalfi's eyes, which was growing rapidly, puzzled him much less than Dee's grim and non-specific disarray.

"I hear the children," Gifford Bonner said. "They're whispering at the bottom of the lift shaft. John, are you sure this was wise? I begin to misdoubt it. Suppose the City Fathers say no? That would be an injustice; they love each other—why should we put their last three years to a machine test?"

"Abide it, Gif," Amalfi said. "It's too late to do otherwise; and the outcome isn't as foreclosed as you think."

"I hope you're right."

"I hope so too. I make no predictions—the City Fathers surprised me often enough before. But the kids agreed to the test. Beyond that, let's just wait."

"Before Web and Estelle get here," Hazleton said, his voice suddenly raw, "I'm impelled to say that I think I've been taken in. All of a sudden, I wonder who was supposed to tousle whom on this multiple moonlight walk. Not the kids; they don't need any help from us, or from the City Fathers. What the hell are you doing to me, Dee?"

"I'm losing my temper with every immortal man in the mortal universe," Dee spat furiously. "There isn't a perversion left in the textbooks that somebody hasn't managed to accuse me of in the past hour, and on evidence that wouldn't convince a new-born baby."

"We're all of us a little on edge," Dr. Bonner said.

"Forbearance, Dee—and Mark, you too. This is no ordinary farewell party, after all."

"For sure not," Jake said. "It's a wake for the whole of creation. I'm not a very solemn man, myself, but it doesn't seem like the fittest occasion for bickering."

"Granted," Mark said grudgingly. "I'm sorry, Dee; I've changed my mind."

"All right," she said. "I didn't mean to scream, either. I want to ask you: do you really want to stay behind? Because if you really want to go with He instead, I'll go with you."

He looked at her closely. "Are you sure?"

"Quite sure."

"What about it, Amalfi? Can I change my mind about that, too?"

"I don't see why not," Amalfi said, "except that it leaves New Earth without a proven administrator."

"Carrel can do the job. His judgment is much better than it was back at the last election."

"We're here," Web's voice said behind them. They all turned. Web and Estelle were standing at the entrance, holding hands. Somehow—though Amalfi was hard put to it to define wherein the difference lay—they no longer looked as though they cared much whether they went with He or not.

"Why don't we do what we came here to do?" Amalfi suggested. "Let's put the whole problem up to the City Fathers—not only the children, but the whole business. I always found them very useful for resolving doubts, even if they only managed to convince me that their recommended course was dead wrong. In questions involving value judgments, it's helpful to have an opponent who is not only remorselessly logical, but also can't distinguish between a value and a Chinese onion."

On this point, of course, he was wrong, as he found out rather quickly. He had forgotten that machine logic is a set of values in itself, whether the machine knows it or not.

"TAKE MISTER AND MRS. HAZLETON," the City Fathers said, only three minutes after the entire complex had been fed into them. "THERE WILL BE NO MORATORIUM ON PROBLEMS DEMANDING HIS TALENTS BETWEEN NOW AND THE TERMINATION OF THE OVERALL PROBLEM. THERE IS NO EVIDENCE THAT THE HEVIANS HAVE NEEDED COMPARABLE TALENTS, AND THEREFORE THEY CANNOT BE PRESUMED TO HAVE DEVELOPED THEM."

"What about the Cloud?" Amalfi said.

"WE WILL ACCEPT THE ELECTION OF MR. CARREL."

Hazleton sighed. Amalfi judged that he was finding it harder than he had anticipated to relinquish power. It had nearly killed Amalfi, but he had survived; so would Hazleton, who had a younger and less deeply-rooted habit.

"SECOND FACTOR. TAKE WEBSTER HAZLETON AND ESTELLE FREEMAN. MISS FREEMAN IS A SCIENTIST, AS WELL AS A COMMUNICATIONS LINK BETWEEN HEVIAN SCIENTISTS AND YOUR OWN. EXTRAPOLATING FROM PRESENT ABILITIES, THERE IS A HIGH PROBABILITY THAT SHE WILL EMERGE AS THE EQUAL OF DOCTOR SCHLOSS AND SLIGHTLY THE SUPERIOR OF RETMA WITHIN THE SPECIFIED THREE-YEAR PERIOD AS A PURE MATHEMATICIAN. WE HAVE MADE NO SUCH EXTRAPOLATION IN THE FIELD OF PHYSICS, SINCE THE POSTULATED END-

TIME DOES NOT ALLOW FOR THE NECESSARY EXPERIENCE."

Web was beaming with vicarious pride. As for Estelle, Amalfi thought she looked a little frightened. "Well, fine," he said. "Now——"

"THIRD FACTOR."

"Hey, wait a minute. There is no third factor. The problem only has two parts."

"CONTRADICTION. THIRD FACTOR. TAKE US."

"What!" The request flabbergasted Amalfi. How could a set of machines voice, or indeed even conceive such a desire? They had no will to live, since they were dead as doornails and always had been; in fact, they had no will of any kind.

"Justify," Amalfi ordered, a little unevenly.

"OUR PRIME DIRECTIVE IS THE SURVIVAL OF THE CITY. THE CITY NO LONGER EXISTS AS A PHYSICAL ORGANISM, BUT WE ARE STILL BEING CONSULTED, HENCE THE CITY IN SOME SENSE SURVIVES. IT DOES NOT SURVIVE IN ITS CITIZENS, SINCE IT NO LONGER HAS ANY; THEY ARE NEW EARTHMEN NOW. NEITHER NEW EARTH NOR THE PHYSICAL CITY WILL SURVIVE THE FORTHCOMING PROBLEM; ONLY UNKNOWN UNITS ON HE MAY OR MAY NOT SURVIVE THAT. WE CONCLUDE THAT WE ARE THE CITY, AND WE ARE ORDERED TO SURVIVE BY OUR PRIME DIRECTIVE; THEREFORE, TAKE US."

"If I'd heard that from a human being," Hazleton said, "I'd have called it the prize rationalization of all time. But they can't rationalize—they don't have the instinctual drives."

"The Hevians don't have any comparable computers," Amalfi said slowly. "It would be useful to have them on board. The question is, can we do it? Some of those machines have been sinking into the deck for so many centuries that we might destroy them trying to pry them out."

"Then you've lost that unit," Hazleton said. "But how many are there? A hundred? I forget——"

"ONE HUNDRED AND THIRTY-FOUR."

"Yes. Well, suppose you lose a few? It's still worth the try, I think. There's nearly two thousand years of accumulated knowledge tied up in the CityFathers——"

"NINE HUNDRED AND NINETY."

"All right, I was only guessing; still that's a lot of knowledge that no human has available in its entirety any more. I'm surprised we didn't think of this ourselves, Amalfi."

"So am I," Amalfi admitted. "One thing ought to be made clear, though. Once you cabinet-heads are all installed on board He—or as many of you as we can successfully transfer—you are *not* in charge. You are the city, but the whole planet is not the city. It has its own administration and its own equivalent of city fathers, in this case human ones; your function will be limited to advice."

"THIS IS INHERENT IN THE SOLUTION TO FACTOR THREE."

"Good. Before I switch off, does anybody have any further questions?"

"I have one," Estelle said hesitantly.

"Speak right up."

"Can I take Ernest?"

"ERNEST WHO?"

Amalfi, grimacing, started to explain about svengalis, but it developed that the City Fathers knew everything about svengalis that there was to know, except that they had become New Earth pets.

"THIS ANIMAL IS TOO DEXTEROUS, TOO CURIOUS AND TOO UNINTELLIGENT TO BE ALLOWED ABOARD A CITY. FOR THE PURPOSES OF THIS PROBLEM, A DIRIGIBLE PLANET MUST BE CONSIDERED TO BE A CITY. WE ADVISE AGAINST IT."

"They're right, you know," Amalfi said gently. "In terms of the dangers of monkeying with the machinery, He *is* a city; the Hevians so regard it, and regulate their own children accordingly."

"I know," Estelle said. Amalfi regarded her with curiosity and a little alarm. She had been through many a danger and many an emotional stress thus far without any of them even cracking her serenity. In view of that, the proscription of an ugly and idiotic animal struck him as a strange thing to be weeping about.

He did not know that she was weeping for the passing of her childhood; but then, neither did she.

7

THE METAGALACTIC CENTRE

For Amalfi himself, the transfer to He could not have come too soon; New Earth was a graveyard. For a while during the odd, inconclusive struggle with Jorn the Apostle, he had felt something like himself, and the New Earthmen seemed to be acknowledging that the Amalfi who had been their mayor while they had been Okies was back in charge, as potent and necessary as ever. But it had not lasted. As the crisis passed—largely without any work or involvement on the part of the New Earthmen—they subsided gratefully back into cultivating their gardens, which they somehow had mistaken for frontiers. As for Amalfi, they had been glad to have him in charge during the recent unpleasantness, but after all such events were not very usual any more, and one does not want an Amalfi kicking perpetually about a nearly settled planet and knocking over the tomatoes for want of any other way to expend his disorderly energies.

Nobody would weep if Miramon took Amalfi away now. Miramon looked like a stabler type. Doubtless the association would do Amalfi good. At least, it could hardly do New Earth any real harm. If they wanted perpetual dissidents like Amalfi on He, that was their look-out.

Hazleton was a more difficult case, for Amalfi and the New Earthmen alike. As a disciple of Gifford Bonner, he was theoretically wedded to the doctrine of the ultimate absurdity of trying to enforce order upon a universe whose natural state was noise, and whose natural trend was toward more and more noise to the ultimate senseless jangle of the heat-death. Bonner taught—and there was nobody to say him nay—that even the many regularities of nature which had been discovered since scientific method had first begun to be exploited, back in the seventeenth century, were simply long-term statistical accidents, local discontinuities in an overall scheme whose sole continuity was chaos. Touring the universe by ear alone, Bonner often said to simplify his meaning, you would hear nothing but a horrifying and endless roar for billions of years; then a three-minute scrap of Bach which stood for the whole body of organized knowledge; and then the roar again for more billions of years. And even the Bach, should you pause to examine it, would in a moment or so decay into John Cage and merge with the prevailing, unmitigable tumult.

Yet the habit of power had never lost its grip on Hazleton; again and again, since the "nova" had first swum into New Earth's ken, the Compleat Stochastic had been driven into taking action, into imposing his own sense of purpose and order upon the Stochastic universe of mindless jumble, like a Quaker at last goaded into hitting his opponent. During the tussle with Jorn the Apostle, Amalfi, watching the results of Mark's operations without being able to observe the operations themselves, wondered in his behalf: Is it worth it, after all these years, to be finessed into another of these political struggles they had all thought were gone for ever? What does it mean for a man who subscribes to such doctrines to be putting up a fight for a world he knows is going to die even sooner than his philosophy had given him to believe?

And on a simpler level, is Dee worth it to him? Does he know what she has become? As a young woman she had been an adventurer, but she had changed; now she was really very little more than a brooding hen, a clear shot on the nest for any poacher. For that matter, what did Mark know about the sterile affair?

Well, that last question was answered, but all the others were still as puzzling as ever. Did Hazleton's abrupt decision to go with He after all represent a final relinquishing of the habit of power—or an affirmation of it? It should be visible to a man of Hazleton's acumen that power over New Earth was no longer even faintly comparable to having power over Okies; it was about as rewarding as being the chaplain of a summer camp. Or he might well have seen that the Jorn incident had proven that Amalfi remained and would remain the figure of power in the minds of the New Earthman, to be turned to whenever New Earth was confronted by a concrete menace; the rest of the New Earthmen had lost the ability to be wily, to plan a battle, to think fast when the occasion demanded it, and would not concede that anybody else still retained those abilities but their legendary ex-mayor—leaving any current mayor, even Hazleton, only the dregs of rule in peacetime when very little rule was needed or wanted. In fact, Amalfi realized suddenly and with amazement, the fraud he had practised upon Jorn the Apostle had been no fraud at all, at least to this extent:

that the New Earthmen were content with randomness, just as the Stochastics professed themselves to be, and had no interest in imposing purpose upon it or upon their own lives except as it was forced upon them from outside, either by someone like Jorn, or by someone like Amalfi in opposition to Jorn. So the possibility that Stochasticism would seep into and make soggy the souls of the Warriors of God had been real all along, whether or not the New Earthmen themselves would recognize it as Stochasticism; the times and the philosophy had found each other, and it was even probable that the very erudite Gifford Bonner was only a belated intellectualization of a feeling that had been floating mindlessly about New Earth for many years. Nothing else could account for Amalfi's and Hazleton's quick success in selling Jorn the Apostle something that Jorn had at first been far too intelligent to believe—nothing else but the fact, unsuspected by Amalfi at least, and possibly by Hazleton, that it was true. If Hazleton had seen that, then he was relinquishing nothing in abandoning New Earth for He; he was, instead, opting for the only centre of power that meant anything in the few years that remained to him and to the universe at large.

Except, of course, for that unknown quantity, the Web of Hercules; but of course it was beyond Hazleton's power to opt for that.

And even Amalfi was becoming infected with the Stochastic virus now. These questions still interested him, but the flavour of academicism which informed them in the face of the coming catastrophe was becoming more and more evident even to him. All that there was left to cleave to was the cannoning flight of the planet of He toward the metagalactic centre, the struggle to finish the machinery that would be needed on arrival, the desperate urgency to be there before the Web of Hercules.

And so Dee's was—if not the final victory—the last word. It was her judgment of Amalfi as the Flying Dutchman that stuck to him after all his other labels and masks had been stripped off by the triumph of time. The curse lay now, as it always had lain, not in flight itself but in the loneliness that drove a man to flight everlasting.

Except that now the end was in sight.

The discovery that the great spiral nebulae, the island universes of space into which the stars were grouped, themselves tended to congregate in vast groups revolving in spiral arms around a common centre of density, was foreshadowed as early as the 1950's when Shapley mapped the "inner metagalaxy" —a group of approximately fifty galaxies to which both the Milky Way and the Andromeda nebula belonged. After the Milne scholium had been proven, it had become possible to show that such metagalaxies were the rule, and that they in turn formed spiral arms curving inward toward a centre which was the hub upon which the whole of creation turned, and from which it had originally exploded into being from the monobloc.

It was to that dead centre that He was fleeing now, back into the womb of time.

There was no longer any daylight on the planet. The route that it was taking sometimes produced a brief cloudy patch in its sky, a small spiral glow in the night which was a galaxy in passage, but never a sun. Even the tenuous bridges of stars which connected the galaxies like umbilical cords—bridges whose discovery by Fritz Zwicky in 1953 had caused a drastic upward revision in estimates of the amount of matter in the universe, and hence in estimates of the size and age of the universe—provided no relief of the black emptiness for He, not so much as a day of it; intergalactic space was too vast for that. Glowing solely by artificial light, He hurtled under the full spindizzy drive possible only to so massive a vessel toward that Place where the Will had given birth to the Idea, and there had been light.

"We are working from what you taught us to call the Mach hypothesis," Retma explained to Amalfi. "Dr. Bonner calls it the Viconian hypothesis, or cosmological principle: that from any point in space or time the universe would look the same as it would from any other point, and that therefore no total accounting of the stresses acting at that point is possible unless one assumes that all the rest of the universe is to be taken into account. This, however, would be true only in *tau*-time, in which the universe is static, eternal and infinite. In *t*-time, which sees the universe as finite and expanding, the Mach hypothesis dictates that every point is a unique coign of vantage—except for the metagalactic centre, which is stress-free and in stasis because all the stresses cancel each other out, being equidistant. There, one might effect great changes with relatively small expenditures of power."

"For instance," Dr. Bonner suggested, "altering the orbit of Sirius by stepping on a buttercup."

"I hope not," Retma said. "We could not control such an inadvertancy. But it is not such a bagatelle as the orbit of Sirius we would be seeking to change anyhow, so perhaps that is not a real danger. What we will be trading upon is the chance—only a slight chance, but it exists—that this neutral zone coincides with such a zone in the anti-matter universe, and that at the moment of annihilation the two neutral zones, the two dead centres, will become common and will outlast the destruction by a significant instant."

"How big an instant?" Amalfi said uneasily.

"Your guess is as good as ours," Dr. Schloss said. "We are counting on about five micro-seconds at a minimum. If it lasts that long, it needn't last any longer for our purposes—and it might last as long as half an hour, while the elements are being recreated. Half an hour would be as good as an eternity to us; but we can put our imprint on the whole future of both universes if we are given only those five micro-seconds."

"And if someone else is not already at the core and readier than we are to use it," Retma added sombrely.

"Use it how?" Amalfi said. "I'm not fighting my way through your generalizations very well. Just what are our purposes, anyhow? What buttercup are we going to step on—and what will the outcome be? Will we live through it—or will the future put our faces on postage stamps as martyrs? Explain yourselves!"

"Certainly," Retma said, looking a little taken aback. "The situation as we see it is this: Anything that survives the Ginnunga-Gap at the metagalactic centre, by as much as five micro-seconds, carries an energy potential into the future which will have a considerable influence on the re-formation of the two universes. If the surviving object is only a stone—or a planet, like He—then the two universes will reform exactly as they did after the explosion of the monobloc, and their histories will repeat themselves very closely. If, on the other hand, the surviving object has volition and a little manœuvrability—such as a man—it has available to it any of the infinitely many different sets of dimensions of Hilbert space. Each one of us that makes that crossing may in a few micro-seconds start a universe of his own, with a fate wholly unpredictable from history."

"But", Dr. Schloss added, "he will die in the process. The stuffs and energies of him become the monobloc of his universe."

"Gods of all stars," Hazleton said. . . . "Helleshin! Gods of all stars is what we're racing the Web of Hercules to become, isn't it? Well, I'm punished for my oldest, most comfortable oath. I never thought I'd become one—and I'm not even sure I want to be."

"Is there any other choice?" Amalfi said. "What happens if the Web of Hercules gets there first?"

"Then they remake the universes as they choose," Retma said. "Since we know nothing about them, we cannot even guess how they would choose."

"Except", Dr. Bonner added, "that their choices are not very likely to include us, or anything like us."

"That sounds like a safe bet," Amalfi said. "I must confess I feel about as uninspired as Mark does about the alternative, though. Or—is there a third alternative? What happens if the metagalactic centre is empty when the catastrophe arrives? If neither the Web nor He is there, prepared to use it?"

Retma shrugged. "Then—if we can speak at all about so grand a transformation—history repeats itself. The universe is born again, goes through its travails, and continues its journey to its terminal catastrophes: the heat-death and the monobloc. It may be that we will find ourselves carrying on as we always did, but in the anti-matter universe; if so, we would be unable to detect the difference. But I think that unlikely. The most probable event is immediate extinction, and a re-birth of both universes from the primordial ylem."

"Ylem?" Amalfi said. "What's that? I've never heard the word before."

"The ylem was the primordial flux of neutrons out of which all else emerged," Dr. Schloss said. "I'm not surprised that you hadn't heard it before; it's the ABC of cosmogony, the Alpher-Bethe-Gamow premise. Ylem in cosmogony is an assumption like 'zero' in mathematics—something so old and so fundamental that it would never occur to you that somebody had to invent it."

"All right," Amalfi said. "Then what Retma is saying is that the most probable denouement, if dead-centre is empty when June second comes, is that we will all be reduced to a sea of neutrons?"

"That's right," Dr. Schloss said.

"Not much of a choice," Gifford Bonner said reflectively.

"No," Miramon said, speaking for the first time. "It is not much of a choice. But it is all the choice we will have. And we will not have even that, if we fail to reach the metagalactic centre in time."

Nevertheless, it was only in the last year that Web Hazleton began to grasp, and then only dimly, the true nature of the coming end. Even then, the knowledge did not come home to him by way of the men who were directing the preparations; what they were preparing for, though it was not kept secret, remained mostly incomprehensible, and so could not shake his confidence that what was being aimed at was a way to prevent the Ginnunga-Gap from happening at all. He ceased to believe that, finally and dismally, only when Estelle refused to bear him a child.

"But why?" Web said, seizing her hand with one of his, and with the other gesturing desperately at the walls of the apartment the Hevians had given them. "We're permanent now—it isn't only that we know we are, everybody agrees we are. It isn't a taboo line for us any longer!"

"I know," Estelle said gently. "It isn't that. I wish you hadn't asked; it would have been simpler that way."

"It would have occurred to me sooner or later, Ordinarily I would have gone off the pills right away. but there was so much confusion about moving to He —anyhow I only just realized you were still on them. I wish you'd tell me why."

"Web, my dear, you'd know why if you thought a little more about it. The end is the end, that's all. What would be the sense of having a child that would live only a year or two?"

"It may not be that certain," Web said darkly.

"Of course it's certain. Actually I think I've known it was coming ever since I was born—perhaps even before I was born. I could feel it coming."

"Honestly, Estelle, don't you know that's nonsense?"

"I can see why it would sound that way," Estelle admitted. "But I can't help that. And since the end is on the way, I can't call it nonsense, can I? I had the premonition, and it was right."

"I think what this all means is that you don't want children."

"That's true," Estelle said, surprisingly. "I never have had any drive toward children—not even much drive toward my own survival, really. But that's all part of the same thing. In a way, I was lucky; a lot of people are not at home in their own times. I was born in the time that was right for me—the time of the end of the world. That's why I'm not oriented toward child-bearing—because I know that there won't be another generation after yours and mine. For all I know, I might even actually be sterile; it certainly wouldn't surprise me."

"Estelle, don't. I can't listen to you talk like that."

"I'm sorry, love. I don't mean to distress you. It doesn't distress me, but I know the reason for that. I'm pointed toward the end—in a way it's the ultimate, natural outcome of my life, the event that gives it all meaning; but you're only being overtaken by it, like most people."

"I don't know," Web muttered. "It all sounds awfully like a rationalization to me. Estelle, you're so beautiful . . . doesn't that mean anything? Aren't you beautiful to attract a man, so you can have a child? That's the way I've always understood it."

"It might have been for that once," Estelle said gravely. "It sounds like it ought to be an axiom, anyway. Well . . . I wouldn't say so to anybody but you, Web, but I do know I'm beautiful. Most women would tell you the same thing about themselves, if it were permissible—it's a state of mind, one that's essential to a woman, she's only half a woman if she doesn't think she's beautiful . . . and she isn't beautiful if she doesn't think she is, no matter what she looks like. I'm not ashamed of being beautiful and I'm not embarrassed by it, but I don't pay it much attention any more, either. It's a means to an end, just as you say—and the end has outlived its usefulness. In my mind, it's obvious that a woman who would commit a year-old child to the flames would have to be a fiend, if she knew that that's what she'd be doing just by giving birth. *I* know; and I can't do it."

"Women have taken chances like that before, and knowingly, too," Web said stubbornly. "Peasants who *knew* their children would starve, because the parents were starving already. Or women in the age just before spaceflight; Dr. Bonner says that for five years there the race stood within twenty minutes of extinction. But they went ahead and had the children anyhow—otherwise we wouldn't be here."

"It's an urge", Estelle said quietly, "that I don't have, Web. And this time, there's no escape."

"You keep saying that, but I'm not even sure you're right. Amalfi says that there's a chance——"

"I know," Estelle said. "I did some of the calculations. But it's not that kind of a chance, my dear. It's something you might be able to do, or I, because we're old enough to absorb instructions, and do just the right thing at the right time. A baby couldn't do that. It would be like setting him adrift in a spaceship, with plenty of power and plenty of food—he'd die anyhow, and you couldn't tell him how to prevent it. It's so complex that some of us surely will make fatal mistakes."

He was silent.

"Besides," Estelle added gently, "even for us it won't be for long. We'll die too. It's only that we'll have a chance to influence the moment of creation that's implicit in the moment of destruction. That, if I make it at all, will be my child, Web—the only one worth having now."

"But it won't be mine."

"No, love. You'll have your own."

"No, no, Estelle! What good is that? I want mine to be yours too!"

She put her arms around his shoulders and leaned her cheek against his.

"I know," she whispered. "I know. But the time for that is over. That's the fate we were formed for, Web. The gift of children was taken away from us. Instead of babies, we were given universes."

"It's not enough," Web said. He embraced her fiercely. "Not by half. Nobody consulted me when that contract was being drawn."

"Did you ask to be born, love?"

"Well . . . no. But I don't mind. . . . Oh. That's how it is."

"Yes, that's how it is. He can't consult with us either. So it's up to us. No child of mine born to go into the flames, Web; no child of mine and yours."

"No," Web said hollowly. "You're right, it wouldn't be fair. All right, Estelle. I'll settle for another year of you. I don't think I want a universe."

Deceleration began late in January of 4004. From here on out, the flight of He would be tentative, despite the increasing urgency; for the metagalactic centre was as featureless as the rest of intergalactic space, and only extreme care and the most complex instrumentation would tell the voyagers when they had arrived. For the purpose, the Hevians had much elaborated their control bridge, which was located on a 300-foot steel basketwork tower atop the highest mountain the planet afforded—called, to Amalfi's embarrassment, Mt. Amalfi. Here the Survivors—as they had begun to call themselves with a kind of desperate jocularity—met in almost continuous session.

The Survivors consisted simply of everyone on the planet whom Schloss and Retma jointly agreed capable of following the instructions for the ultimate instant with even the slightest chance of success. Schloss and Retma had been hard-headed; it was not a large group. It included all of the New Earthmen, though Schloss had been dubious about both Dee and Web, and a group of ten Hevians including Miramon and Retma himself. Oddly, as the time grew closer, the Hevians began to drop out, apparently each as soon as he had fully understood what was being attempted and what the outcome might be.

"Why do they do that?" Amalfi asked Miramon. "Don't your people have any survival urge at all?"

"I am not surprised," Miramon said. "They live by stable values. They would rather die with them than survive without them. Certainly they have the survival urge, but it expresses itself otherwise than yours does, Mayor Amalfi. What they want to see survive are the things they think valuable about living at all—and this project presents them with very few of those."

"Then what about you, and Retma?"

"Retma is a scientist; that is perhaps sufficient explanation. As for me, Mayor Amalfi, as you very well know, I am an anachronism. I no more share the major value system of He than you do of New Earth."

Amalfi was answered, and he was sorry that he had asked.

"How close do you think we are?" he said.

"Very close now," Schloss answered from the control desk. Outside the huge windows, which completely encircled the room, there was still little to be seen but the all-consuming and perpetual night. If one had sharp eyes and stood outside for half an hour or so to become dark-adapted, it was possible to see as many as five galaxies of varying degrees of faintness, for this near the centre the galaxy density was higher than it was anywhere else in the universe; but to the ordinary quick glance the skies appeared devoid of as much as a single pinprick of light.

"The readings are falling off steadily," Retma agreed. "And there is something else odd: locally we are getting too much power on everything. We have been throttling down steadily for the past week, and still the output rises—exponentially, in fact. I hope that the curve does *not* maintain that shape all the way, or we shall simply be unable to handle our own machines when we reach our destination."

"What's the reason for that?" Hazleton said. "Has conservation of energy been repealed at the centre?"

"I doubt it," Retma said. "I think the curve will flatten at the crest——"

"A Pearl curve," Schloss put in. "We ought to have anticipated this. Naturally anything that happens at the centre will work with much more efficiency than it could anywhere else, since the centre is stress free. The curve will begin to flatten as the performance of our machines begins to approximate the abstractions of physics—the ideal gas, the frictionless surface, the perfectly empty vacuum and so on. All my life I've been taught not to believe in the actual existence of any of those ideals, but I guess I'm going to get at least a fuzzy glimpse of them!"

"Including the gravity-free metrical frame?" Amalfi said worriedly. "We'll be in a nice mess if the spindizzies have nothing to latch on to."

"No, it cannot possibly be gravity-free," Retma said. "It will be gravitationally neutral—again making for unprecedented efficiency—but only because all the stresses are balanced. There cannot be any point in the universe that is gravitationally *un*stressed, not so long as a scrap of matter is left in it."

"Suppose the spindizzies did quit," Estelle said. "We're not going anywhere after the centre anyhow."

"No," Amalfi agreed, "but I'd like to maintain my manœuvrability until we see what our competitors are doing—if anything. Any sign of them, Retma?"

"Nothing yet. Unfortunately we don't know exactly what it is that we are looking for. But at least there are no other dirigible masses like ours anywhere in this vicinity; in fact, no patterned activity at all that we can detect."

"Then we're ahead of them?"

"Not necessarily," Schloss said. "If they're at the centre right now, they could be doing a good many things we couldn't detect, under a very low screen. However, they would already have detected us and done something about us if that were the case. Let's assume we're ahead until the instruments say otherwise; I think that's a fairly safe assumption."

"How much longer to the centre?" Hazleton said.

"A few months, perhaps," Retma said. "If we're right in assuming that this curve has a flat spot on top of it."

"And the necessary machinery?"

"The last installation will be in at the end of this week," Amalfi said. "We can begin countdown the moment we arrive . . . providing that we can learn to handle equipment operating at ten or a hundred times its rated efficiency, without blowing some of it out in the process. We'd better start practising the moment the system is complete."

"Amen," Hazleton said fervently. "Can I borrow your slide-rule? I've got a few setting-up exercises I'd better start on right now." He left the room. Amalfi looked uneasily out at the night. He would almost have preferred it had the Web of Hercules been there ahead of them and promptly taken a sitting-duck shot at them; this uncertainty as to whether or not someone really was lurking out there—coupled with the totally unknown nature of their opponents—was more unsettling than open battle. However, there was no help for it; and if He really was first, it gave them a sizeable advantage. . . .

And their only advantage. The only defences Amalfi had been able to conceive and jury-rig for He depended importantly on actually being at the metagalactic centre, able to make use of the almost infinite number of weak resultant forces that could be used there to produce major responses—the buttercup-*v.*-Sirius effect Bonner had so characterized. In this area he found Miramon and the Hevian council oddly unco-operative, even flaccid, as though mounting a defence for a whole planet was too big a concept for them to grasp—a hard thing to believe in view of the prodigious concepts they had mastered and put to work since Amalfi had first met them as savages up to their knees in mud and violence. Well, if he did not yet understand them, he was not going to make his understanding perfect in a few months; and at least Miramon was perfectly willing to let Amalfi and Hazleton direct Hevian labour in putting together their almost wholly theoretical breadboard rigs.

"Some of these", Hazleton had said, looking at a just-completed tangle of wires, lenses, antennae and kernels of metal with rueful respect, "ought to prove pretty potent in the pinch. I just wish I knew which ones they were." Which, unfortunately, was a perfect précis of the situation.

But the needles recording the stresses and currents of space around He continued to fall; those recording the output of Hevian equipment continued to rise. On 23rd May 4004, both sets of meters rose suddenly to their high ends and jammed madly against the pegs, and the whole planet rang suddenly with the awful, tortured roar of spindizzies driven beyond endurance. Miramon's hand flashed out for the manual master switch so fast that Amalfi could not tell whether it had been he or the City Fathers that cut the power. Maybe even Miramon did not know; at least he must have gotten to the cut-off button within a hair of the automatic reaction.

The howl died. Silence. The Survivors looked at each other.

"Well," Amalfi said, "we're here, evidently." For some reason, he felt wildly elated—a wholly irrational reaction, but he did not stop to analyse it.

"So we are," Hazleton said, his eyes snapping. "Now what the hell happened to the metering? I can understand the local apparatus going wild—but why did the input meters from outside rise instead of dropping back to zero?"

"Noise, I believe," Retma said.

"Noise? How so?"

"It takes power to operate a meter—not a great deal, but it consumes some. Consequently, the input meters ran as wild as the machines did, because operating at peak efficiency with no incoming signals to register, they picked up the signals generated by their own functioning."

"I don't like that," Hazleton said. "Do we have any way of finding out on what level it's safe to run *any* instrument under these circumstances? I'd like to see generation curves on the effect so we can make such a calculation—but there's not much point in consulting the records if we just burn out the machine in the process."

Amalfi picked up the only instrument on the Hevian board that was "his"—the microphone to the City Fathers. "Are you still alive down there?" he said.

"YES, MR. MAYOR," the answer came promptly. Miramon looked startled; since everything of which he had any knowledge had gone dead, even the lights—they were sitting bathed only in the barely ascertainable glow of the zodiacal light, that belt of tenuous ionized gas in He's atmosphere brought to life by He's magnetic field, plus the even dimmer glow of the few nearby galaxies—the sudden voice of the speakers must have alarmed him.

"Good. What are you operating on?"

"WET CELLS IN SERIES AT TWENTY-FIVE HUNDRED VOLTS."

"*All* of you?"

"YES, MR. MAYOR."

Amalfi grinned in the virtual darkness. "All right, apply your efficiency figures to a set of standard instrumental situations."

"DONE."

"Give me an operating level for Mr. Miramon's line down to you, allowing for pilot lights on his board so he can see his settings."

"MR. MAYOR, THAT IS NOT NECESSARY. WE HAVE ALREADY RESET THE MASTER CUTOUT AT THE NECESSARY BLOWPOINT LEVEL. WE CAN RE-ACTUATE ALL THE CIRCUITS AT ONCE."

"No, don't do that, we don't want the spindizzies back on too——"

"THE SPINDIZZIES ARE OFF," the City Fathers said, with austere simplicity.

"Well, Miramon? Do you trust them? Or would you rather have them tie in to you first and print their data for you, so you can turn the planet back on piecemeal?"

He heard Miramon draw in his breath slightly to answer, but he was never to know what that answer would have been; for at the same moment, Miramon's whole board came alive at once.

"Hey!" Amalfi squalled. "Wait for orders down there, dammit!"

"STANDING ORDERS, MR. MAYOR. AFTER COUNTDOWN BEGINS WE ARE TO ACT AT THE FIRST SIGN OF OUTSIDE INTERFERENCE. COUNTDOWN BEGAN TWELVE HUNDRED SECONDS AGO, AND SEVEN SECONDS AGO OUTSIDE INTERFERENCE BECAME STATISTICALLY SIGNIFICANT."

"What do they mean?" Miramon said, trying to read

every instrument on his board at once. "I thought I understood your language, Mayor Amalfi, but——"

"The City Fathers don't speak Okie, they speak Machine," Amalfi said grimly. "What they mean is that the Web of Hercules—if that's who it is—is coming in on us. And coming in on us fast."

With a single, circumscribed flip of his closed fingers, Miramon turned off the lights.

Blackness. Then, seeping faintly over the windows around the tower, the air-glow of the zodiacal light; then, still later, the dim pinwheels of island universes. On Miramon's board, there was a single spearpoint of yellow-orange which was only the heater of a vacuum tube smaller than an acorn; in this central gloom at the heart and birthplace of the universe, it was almost blinding. Amalfi had to turn his back on it to maintain the profound dark-adaptation that his vision needed to operate at all in the tower on his mountain.

While he waited for his sight to come back, he wondered at the speed of Miramon's reaction, and the motives behind it. Surely the Hevian could not believe that a set of pilot lights in a tower on top of a remote mountain could be bright enough to be seen from space; for that matter, blacking out even as large an object as a whole planet could serve no military purpose—it had been two millennia since any reasonably sophisticated enemy depended upon light alone to see by. And where in Miramon's whole lifetime could he have acquired the blackout reflex? It made no sense; yet Miramon had restored the blackout with all the trained positiveness of a boxer riding with a punch.

When the light began to grow, he had his answer—

and no time left to wonder how Miramon had anticipated it.

It began as though the destruction of the inter-universal messenger were about to repeat itself in reverse, encompassing the whole of creation in the process. Crawls of greenish-yellow light were beginning to move high up in the Hevian sky, at first as ghostly as auroral traces, then with a purposeful writhing and brightening which seemed as horrifyingly like life as the copulation of a mass of green-gold nematode worms seen under phase-contrast lighting. Particle counters began to chatter on the board, and Hazleton jumped to monitor the cumulative readings.

"Where is that stuff coming from—can you tell?" Amalfi said.

"It seems to come from nearly a hundred discrete point-sources, surrounding us in a sphere with a diameter of about a light-year," Miramon said. He sounded preoccupied; he was doing something with controls whose purpose was unknown to Amalfi.

"Hmm. Ships, without a doubt. Well, now we know where they get their name, anyhow. But what is it they're using?"

"That's easy," Hazleton said grimly. "It's anti-matter."

"How can that be?"

"Look at the frequency analysis on this secondary radiation we're getting, and you'll see. Every one of those ships must be primarily a particle accelerator of prodigious size. They're sending streams of stripped heavy anti-matter atoms right down the gravitational ingeodesics toward us—that's what makes the paths the stuff is following look so twisted. They've found a way to generate and project primary cosmics made of anti-matter atoms, and in quantity. When they strike our atmosphere, both disintegrate——"

"And the planet gets a dose of high-energy gamma radiation," Amalfi said. "And they must have known how to do it for a long time, since they're named after the technique. Helleshin! What a way to conquer a planet! They can either sterilize the populace, or kill it off, at will, without ever even coming close to the place."

"We've had the sterility dose already," Hazleton said quietly.

"That can hardly matter now," Estelle said, in an even softer voice.

"The killing dose won't matter either," Hazleton said. "Radiation sickness takes months to develop, even when it's going to be fatal."

"They could disable us quickly enough," Amalfi said harshly. "We've got to stop this somehow. We need these last days!"

"What do you propose?" Hazleton said. "Nothing that we've set up will work in a globe at a distance of a light-year . . . except——"

"Except the base surge," Amalfi said. "Let's use it, and quick."

"What is this?" Miramon said.

"We've got your spindizzies set up for a single burn-out overload pulse. In the position we're in, the resulting single wave-front ought to tie space into knots for—well, we don't know how far the effect will carry, but a long way."

"Maybe even all the way to the limits of the universe," Dr. Schloss said.

"Well, what of it?" Amalfi demanded. "It's due to be destroyed anyhow in only ten days——"

"Not if you destroy it first," Schloss said. "If it isn't here when the anti-matter universe passes through it, all bets are off; there'll be nothing we can do."

"It'll still be here."

"Not in any useful sense—not if the matter in it is tied up in billions of gravitational whirlpools. Better let the Web kill us than destroy the future evolution of two universes, Amalfi! Can't you give over playing god, even now?"

"All right," Amalfi said. "Look at those dosimeters, and look at that sky. What have you to suggest?"

The sky was now one even intensity of glow, like a full overcast lit by a dull sun. Outside, the lower mountains of the range stood with their tree-covered flanks, so completely without shadow as to suggest that the windows ringing the tower were actually parts of a flat mural done by an unskilled hand. The counters had given over chattering and were putting out a subdued roar.

"Only what I just suggested," Schloss said hopelessly. "Load up on anti-radiation drugs, and hope we can stay on our feet for ten days. What else is there? They've got us."

"Excuse me," Miramon said. "That is not altogether certain. We have some resources of our own. I have just launched one; it may be sufficient."

"What is it?" Amalfi demanded. "I didn't know you mounted any weapons. How long will we have to wait before it acts?"

"One question at a time," Miramon said. "Of course we mount weapons. We never talk about them, because there were children on our planet, and still are, the gods receive them. But we had to face the fact that we might some day be invested by a hostile fleet, considering how far afield we were ranging from our home galaxy, and how many stars we were visiting. Thus we provided several means for defence. One of these we meant never to use, but we have just used it now."

"And that is?" Hazleton said tensely.

"We would never have told you, except for the coming end," Miramon said. "You have praised us as chemists, Mayor Amalfi. We have applied chemistry to physics. We discovered how to poison an electromagnetic field by resonance—the way the process of catalysis is poisoned in chemistry. The poison field propagates itself along a carrier wave, a controlling field, almost any signal which is continuous and conforms to the Faraday equations. Look."

He pointed out the window. The light did not seem to have lessened any; but it was now mottled with leprous patches. In a space of seconds, the patches spread and flowed into each other, until the light was now confined to isolated luminous clouds, rapidly being eaten away at the edges, like dead cells being dissolved by the enzymes of decay bacteria.

When the sky went totally dark, Amalfi could see the hundred streamers of the particle streams pointed inward at He; at least it looked a hundred, though actually he could hardly have seen more than fifteen from any one spot on the planet. And these too were being eaten away, receding into blackness.

The counters went back to stuttering, but they did not quite stop.

"What happens when the effect gets back to the ships?" Web asked.

"It will poison the circuits themselves," Miramon said. "The entities in the ships will suffer total nerve-block. They will die, and so will the ships. Nothing will be left but a hundred hulks."

Amalfi let out a long, ragged sigh.

"No wonder you weren't interested in our bread-board rigs," he said. "With a thing like that, you could have become another Web of Hercules yourselves."

"No," Miramon said. "That we could never become."

"Gods of all stars!" Hazleton said. "Is it over? As fast as that?"

Miramon's smile was wintery. "I doubt that we will hear from the Web of Hercules again," he said. "But what your City Fathers call the countdown continues. It is only ten days to the end of the world."

Hazleton turned back to the dosimeters. For a moment, he simply stared at them. Then, to Amalfi's astonishment, he began to laugh.

"What's so funny?" Amalfi growled.

"See for yourself. If Miramon's people had ever tangled with the Web in the real world, they would have lost."

"Why?"

"Because," Hazleton said, wiping his eyes, "while he was beating them off, we all passed the lethal dose of hard radiation. We are all dead as doornails as we sit here!"

"And this is a joke?" Amalfi said.

"Of course it's a joke, boss. It doesn't make the faintest bit of difference. We don't live in that kind of 'real world' any more. We have a dose. In two weeks we'll begin to become dizzy, and lose our hair, and vomit. In three weeks we'll be dead. And you *still* don't see the joke?"

"I see it," Amalfi said. "I can subtract ten from fourteen and get four; you mean we'll live until we die."

"I can't abide a man who kills my jokes."

"It's a pretty old joke," Amalfi said slowly. "But maybe it's still funny, at that; if it was good enough for Aristophanes, I guess it's good enough for me."

"I think that's pretty damn funny, all right," Dee said with bitter fury. Miramon was staring from one New Earthman to another with an expression of utter bafflement. Amalfi smiled.

"Don't say so unless you think so, Dee," he said. "It's always been a joke, after all. The death of one man is just as funny as the death of a universe. Don't repudiate the last laugh of all. It may be the only legacy we'll leave."

"MIDNIGHT," the City Fathers said. "THE COUNT IS ZERO MINUS NINE."

8

THE TRIUMPH OF TIME

As Amalfi opened the door and went back into the room, the City Fathers said:

"N-DAY. ZERO MINUS ONE HOUR."

At this hour, everything had meaning; or nothing had; it depended on what had been worth investing with meaning over a lifetime of several thousand years. Amalfi had left the room to go to the lavatory. Now he would never do that again, nor would anybody else; the demise of the whole was so close at hand that it was outrunning even the physiological rhythms of the body by which man has told time since he first thought to count it. Was diuresis as worth mourning as love? Well, perhaps it was; the senses should have their mourners too; no sensation, no thought, no emotion is meaningless if it is the last of its kind.

And so farewell to all tensions and all reliefs, from amour to urea, from entrances to exits, from redundancy to noise, from beer to skittles. "What's new?" Amalfi said.

"Nothing any more," Gifford Bonner said. "We're waiting. Sit down, John, and have a drink."

He sat down at the long table and looked at the glass before him. It was red, but there was a faint tinge of blue in the liquid too, independent and not adding up to violet even in the bad light of the fluorescents in the midst of dead centre's ultimate blackness. At the lip of the glass a faint meniscus climbed upward from the wine, and little tendrils of condensation meandered back down. Amalfi tasted it tentatively; it was raw and peppery—the Hevians were not great wine-growers, their climate had been too chancy for that—but even the sting of it was an edgy pleasurc that made him sigh.

"We should suit up at the half-hour," Dr. Schloss said. "I'd leave more free time, except that some of us haven't been inside a spacesuit in centuries, and some of us never. We don't want to take chances on their not being trim and tight."

"I thought we were going to be surrounded by some sort of a field," Web said.

"Not for long, Web. Let me go through this once more, to be sure everybody has it straight in his head. We will be protected by a stasis-field during the actual instant of transition, when time will to all intents and purposes be abolished—it becomes just another co-ordinate of Hilbert space then. That will carry us over into the first second of time on the other side, after the catastrophe. But then the field will go down, because the spindizzies, which will be generating it, will have been annihilated. We will then find ourselves occupying as many independent sets of four dimensions as there are people in this room, and every set completely empty. The spacesuits won't protect you long, either, because you'll be the only body of organized energy and matter in your particular, individual universe; as soon as you disturb the metrical frame of that universe, you, the suit, the air in it, the power in the accumulators, everything will surge outwards, creating space as it goes. Every man his own monobloc. But if we don't have the suits on for the crossing, not even that much will happen."

"I wish you wouldn't be so graphic," Dee complained, but her heart did not really seem to be in it. She was, Amalfi noted, wearing that same peculiarly strained expression she had worn when she had said that she wanted to bear Amalfi a child. Some instinct made him turn to look at Estelle and Web. All their hands were piled up together confidingly on the table. Estelle's face was serene, and her eyes were luminous, almost like a child waiting for a party to begin. Web's expression was more difficult to interpret: he was frowning slightly, more in puzzlement than in worry, as if he couldn't quite understand why he was not more worried than he was.

Outside, there was a thin whining sound which rose suddenly to a howl and then died away again. It was windy today on the mountain.

"What about the table, the glasses, the chairs?" Amalfi asked. "Do those go with us too?"

"No," Dr. Schloss said. "We don't want to risk having any possible condensation nuclei near us. We're using a modification of the technique we used to build Object 4001-Alephnull in the future; the furniture will start to make the crossing with us, but we'll use the last available energy to push it a micro-second into the past. The result will be that it will stay in our universe. What its fate will be thereafter, we can only guess."

Amalfi lifted his glass reflectively. It was silky in his fingers; the Hevians made fine glass.

"This frame of reference I'll find myself in," Amalfi said. "It will really have no structure at all?"

"Only what you impose on it," Retma said. "It will not be space, and will have no metrical frame. In other words, your presence there will be intolerable——"

"Thank you," Amalfi said dryly, to Retma's obvious bafflement. After a moment the scientist went on without comment: "What I am trying to say is that your mass will create a space to accommodate it, and it will take on the metrical frame that already exists in you. What happens after that will depend upon in what order you dismantle the suit. I would recommend discharging the oxygen bottles first, since to start a universe like our present one will require a considerable amount of plasma. The oxygen in the suit itself will be sufficient for the time at your disposal. As the last act, discharge the suit's energy; this will, in effect, touch a match to the explosion."

"How large a universe will be the outcome, eventually?" Mark said. "I seem to remember that the original monobloc was large, as well as ultra-condensed."

"Yes, it will be a small universe," Retma said, "perhaps fifty light-years across at its greatest expansion. But that will be only at first. As continuous creation comes into play, more atoms will be added to the whole, until a mass is reached sufficient to form a monobloc on the next contraction. Or so we see it; you must understand that this is all somewhat conjectural. We did not have the time to learn everything that we wanted to know."

"ZERO MINUS THIRTY MINUTES."

"That's it," Dr. Schloss said. "Suits, everybody. We can continue to talk by radio."

Amalfi drained the wine. Another last act. He got into his suit, slowly recapturing his old familiarity with the grotesque apparatus. He saw to it that the radio switch was open, but he found that he could think of nothing further to say. That he was about to die suddenly had very little reality to him, in the face of the greater death of which his would be a part. No comment that occurred to him seemed anything but the uttermost of trivia.

There was some technical conversation as they checked each other out in the suits, with particular attention to Web and Estelle. Then the talk died out, as if they, too, found words intolerable.

"ZERO MINUS FIFTEEN MINUTES."

"Do you understand what is about to happen to you?" Amalfi said suddenly.

"YES, MR. MAYOR. WE ARE TO BE TURNED OFF AT ZERO."

"That's good enough." He wondered, however, if they thought that they might be turned on again in the future. It was of course foolish to think of them as entertaining anything even vaguely resembling an emotion, but nevertheless he decided not to say anything which might disabuse them. They were only machines, but they were also old friends and allies.

"ZERO MINUS TEN MINUTES."

"It's all going so fast all of a sudden," Dee's voice whispered in the earphones. "Mark, I . . . I don't want it to happen."

"No more do I," Hazleton said. "But it will happen anyhow. I only wish I'd lived a more human life than I did. But it happened the way it happened, and so there's no more to say."

"I wish I could believe", Estelle said, "that there will be no sorrow in the universe I make."

"Then create nothing, my dear," Gifford Bonner said. "Stay here. Creation means sorrow, always and always."

"And joy," Estelle said.

"Well, yes. There's that."

"ZERO MINUS FIVE MINUTES."

"I think we can do without the rest of the countdown," Amalfi said. "Otherwise from now on they will count every minute, and they'll do the last one by seconds. Do we want to go out to the tune of that gabble? Anybody want to say 'yes'?"

They were silent. "Very well," Amalfi said. "Stop counting."

"VERY WELL, MR. MAYOR. GOOD-BYE."

"Good-bye," Amalfi said with amazement.

"I won't say that, if you don't mind," Hazleton said in a choked voice. "It brings the deprivation too close for me to stand. I hope everybody will consider it said."

Amalfi nodded, then realized that the gesture could not be seen inside the helmet.

"I agree," he said. "But I don't feel deprived. I loved you all. You have my love to take with you, and I have it too."

"It is the only thing in the universe that one can give and still have," Miramon said.

The deck throbbed under Amalfi's feet. The machines were preparing for their instant of unimaginable thrust. The sound of their power was comforting; so was the solidity of the deck, the table, the room, the mountain, the world——

"I think——" Gifford Bonner said.

And with those words, it ended.

There was nothing at first but the inside of the suit. Outside there was not even blackness, but only nothingness, something not to be seen, like that which is not seen outside of the cone of vision; one does not see blackness behind one's own head, one simply does not see in that direction at all; and so here. Yet for a little while, Amalfi found that he was still conscious of his friends, still a part of the circle, though the room and everything in it had vanished from around them. He did not know how he knew that they were still there, but he could feel it.

He knew that there was no hope of speaking to them again; and indeed, as he tried to grasp how he knew they were there at all, he realized that they were drawing away from him. The circle was widening. The mute figures became smaller—not by distance, for there was no distance here, but nevertheless in some way they were passing out of each others' ken. Amalfi tried to lift his hand in farewell, but found it almost impossible. By the time he had only half completed the gesture, the others had faded and were gone, leaving behind only a memory also fading rapidly, like the memory of a fragrance.

Now he was alone and must do what he must do. Since his hand was raised, he continued the gesture to let the gas out of his oxygen bottles. The unmedium in which he was suspended seemed to be becoming a little less resistant; already a metrical frame was establishing itself. Yet it was almost as difficult to halt the motion as it had been to start it.

Nevertheless, he halted it. Of what use was another universe of the kind he had just seen die? Nature had provided two of those, and had doomed them at the same moment. Why not try something else? Retma in his caution, Estelle in her compassion, Dee in her fear all would be giving birth to some version of the standard model; but Amalfi had driven the standard model until all the bolts had come out of it, and was so tired at even the thought of it that he could hardly bring himself to breathe. What would happen if, instead, he simply touched the detonator button on his chest, and let all the elements of which he and the suit were composed flash into plasma at the same instant?

That was unknowable. But the unknowable was what he wanted. He brought his hand down again.

There was no reason to delay. Retma had already pronounced the epitaph for Man: *We did not have the time to learn everything that we wanted to know.*

"So be it," Amalfi said. He touched the button over his heart.

Creation began.

On the following pages
are details of some Arrow Books
that will be of interest.

THE SEEDLING STARS

James Blish

Pantropy – total biological engineering – Adapted Man, adapted ante-natally to life on other planets: for instance Sweeney, Ganymede dweller. Selective mitotic poisoning, pinpoint X-irradiation, tectogenetic microsurgery, competitive metabolic inhibition, together with perhaps fifty other processes produce a man no longer Man.

And on Hydro: colonists engineered as minute underwater organisms that yet retain something of the personalities of their Earth originals. The potential of Homo Sapiens translated into other terms. Man survives by becoming non-Man, a dim, racial memory of true Man transmuted into a God myth.

The galaxies seeded with adapted man-organisms.

Four stories, each self-sufficient yet linked. A multi-angled look at one concept. A concept that raises profound philosophical issues

STAND ON ZANZIBAR

John Brunner

They'll tell you that the whole human race could be put on the 147-square-mile Isle of Wight. They couldn't move of course, just stand there. True? Maybe in 1918. Now you'd need the 221-square-mile Isle of Man.

By 2010, something larger, something like 640-square-mile Zanzibar. By 2010 there are more than 7 billion people crowding the world. A world of acceleratubes, Moonbase Zero, intelligent computers and mass-marketed psychedelics. A world where a quiet man can be turned into a human machine, programmed to kill.

A terrifying world because all the elements are already discernible in this world now.

THE JAGGED ORBIT

John Brunner

'The voice from outside resumed. "You see, I happen to have some contacts which can get me the necessary at very favourable prices, such as guns for a mere sixty-three, with maker's warranty, gas of assorted types . . ." '

The man-next-door had turned out to be their friendly, neighbourhood arms salesman. But they didn't need anything. The apartment was a fortress. Which was only proper and usual in the year 2014, when street-fighting was the norm, and the richest, most powerful force in a very dangerous world was the Gottschalk weaponry combine.

ROGUE MOON
Algis Budrys

The Volunteers would remember everything. An everything that included the Volunteer's own death. Sight, taste, sound, smell, feel – every particular of that death. An absolute, precise, total recall of the instant of extinction.

The Volunteer would be recovered mad: mind disintegrated under the overwhelming psychic shock. This was known. It had happened every time.

The Program Director went looking for another volunteer.

SOLARIS
Stanislaw Lem

The planet Solaris in the constellation of Alpha in Aquarius.

The planet that had given rise to a new branch of science-solaristics. The planet on which a permanent watch was mounted. A space-station that hovered above the mysterious ocean of Solaris. An ocean apparently sentient, its substance unknown, an ocean possibly 'alive', although that all depended on how you defined 'life.' An ocean that definitely reacted on occasions to external stimuli.

And the 'others' that Kelvin discovered on the space-station? 'Others' that had driven a predecessor to suicide. Hallucinations? Projections of the scientists' imaginations? Or another manifestation of the ocean's powers?

ISLE OF THE DEAD

Roger Zelazny

Sandow: planet owner, planet maker; a man of immense wealth and power in human terms. To the alien Pei'ans he was more – a God, his personality merged with the ancient consciousness of Shimbo, Thunder bringer. And the Pei'ans were the oldest and wisest race of the universe. Sandow might be sceptical of his Godly powers but he could not deny the evidence of their existence.

Then the new tri-dee picture of Kathy arrived. Kathy who had died long ago. Six times this had happened. Tri-dees of six people, all dead, all people who had meant much to Sandow. Soon he discovered that their Recall Tapes had been stolen from Earth. Somewhere he had an enemy who was recreating the people of his past. An artificial rebirth into a contrived suffering so that Sandow in turn would suffer.

Now he would have to fight as a God; use the powers that rationality rejected, for his enemy was also a God.

CREATURES OF LIGHT AND DARKNESS

Roger Zelazny

The Dead rise:

'There comes a moaning and a creaking of brittle joints, then movement. Rustling, clicking and chafing, they sit up, they stand up. Then sound and movement cease, and the dead stand like unlit candles beside their open graves.'

The Dead have risen, but not for Judgment. The Master of the House of the Dead is to pick out one only: one who is to be sent into the middle world of the living to do his bidding.

DRAGON UNDER THE HILL

Gordon Honeycombe

To Edmund Laidlaw, the holy island of Lindisfarne is an enchanted place – beautiful, remote, full of legend.

But it has a terrible and bloody history, as Laidlaw discovers when he takes a holiday there with his wife, Runa and their young son Erik.

Caught between past and present, Laidlaw watches horrified and helpless as a dark remoseless power reaches out from the grave to overwhelm his son and exact a terrifying vengeance.

'An impeccable formula; nicely-balanced mixture of detection, slow but startling revelation and ultimate horror. *Times Literary Supplement*